W9-ADX-958

The Likes of Which

By Eugene Walter

Fiction

Jennie the Watercress Girl

The Untidy Pilgrim

(Lippincott Prize Novel)

Love You Good; See You Later

Poetry

Monkey Poems

Shapes of the River

Singerie-Songerie

Also

Fellini's Satyricon (Translation)

American Cooking: Southern Style

The Dainty Glutton's Handbook

The Likes of Which

Stories by

Eugene Walter

DHP

Decatur House Press
Washington, D.C.

Grateful acknowledgment is made to *The Paris Review, The Transatlantic Review, Botteghe Oscure, Whetstone, The London Magazine, Harper's Magazine,* Doubleday and Co., Ginn and Co., the National Broadcasting Company, Editore Sugar (Milan), *Cronache* (Rome), R.A.I. (Rome), and Ullstein Verlag (Frankfurt) who have published, translated, anthologized, dramatized, and/or broadcast certain of these stories.

Typeset at The Writer's Center, Glen Echo, Maryland, a center supported in part by grants from the National Endowment for the Arts. Printed by Universal LIthographers, Inc., Cockeysville, Maryland.

FIRST EDITION

LIBRARY OF CONGRESS CATALOGING IN PUBLICATION DATA

Walter, Eugene, 1921-
The likes of which.

CONTENTS: I love you Batty sisters.—The charmer.—Careless Willadell.—In the orchard. [etc.]
I. Title.
PZ4.W2318Li [PS3573.A47228] 813'.5'4 79-15518
ISBN 0-916276-06-6

Decatur House Press, Ltd.
2122 Decatur Place, NW
Washington, D.C. 20008

Contents

For Muriel Spark

In the Andreanof Islands I've seen dogs sitting in the snow, bewitched by the playing of the Northern Lights; everywhere I've ever been I've noticed anecdote crystallize into legend and heard hearsay, muddy and shapeless, taking the pure form of myth.

Dr. S. Willoughby, *Vues d'Optiques*, 1926.

The Likes of Which

I Love You Batty Sisters

There were these two sisters in Mobile, you know what two sisters in the South can be, I mean they stayed just sisters, and they spent a lot of time just being sisters, and they were called the Tolliver "Girls" even when they were older than time itself. They were ordinary girls, really, neither pretty nor plain, their dress neither flamboyant nor prim—at first. But they were sisters and *abetted* one another, and there's part of their history.

They lived down on St. Anthony Street, not far from Fresh-Air Charlie. They had beaux, they had young men who came in groups to drink chocolate and sing *I'm the Messenger Boy in Demand* to mandolin accompaniment, and afterwards go on to stronger brew at Klosky's Saloon or more audacious company at Shreveport Sue's.

Their father kept a very good restaurant down on Royal Street, though they scarcely set foot in it, and sold it as soon as he died. He left them pretty well fixed anyway, and what with the money left from the sale of the business, they had a pretty penny, especially for those days. So they thought they'd travel. The St. Louis Exposition was going full blast at the time, so nothing would do but traipse off and come home loaded down with cut glass souvenir cups, and spools of *passementerie.* That's when it was—on their return to Mobile—

that they decided never to return to a place where they'd had a really good time. Of course this brought up big disagreements as to how good a time constituted a good enough time to never go back to any one particular place. Nobody ever knew how they worked it all out, but supposed they had little meetings and voted.

Once they went to Montgomery just when the Jesse French Piano Company was opening a new showroom and music store. Their visit coincided with the opening of a new trolley line. They were both musical, so they sailed right into the Jesse French shop and played *I Want My Chicken Back* with variations, on two pianos. They played with their eyes closed and heads thrown back.

"Chicken?" whispered the wide-eyed manager of the store, staring at their Gainsborough hats. "Ostrich alone, of all the bird kingdom, will suffice these girls."

Their music was so enticing—they were playing crazy quick ragtime—that all the trolleys stopped in the street to listen.

"For music is a precious joy!" cried out Belladair.

"Amen!" said Mary Cross.

So there was another return to Mobile with both sisters flushed and elated and full of things to tell, and there was another place they'd enjoyed themselves, and couldn't go back. Birmingham was soon out of the question, too, not because they liked that city, but because they had cousins in all the little towns on the way, and spent summers of at least two-week stays with all in turn. The fact is, Belladair and Mary Cross were seldom not enjoying themselves. They had a lovely time in New Orleans, staying at the old St. Charles Hotel, and playing at petty shoplifting in the big department stores: spools of colored thread mostly. Soon New Orleans was relegated to recollected pleasure, and Slidell, Bay St. Louis, Pass Christian, Gulfport, Biloxi, Pascagoula, and Gautier each in turn visited, enjoyed, and consigned to memory's lovely limbo.

They'd always detested Atlanta, because of an aunt there, so they did their fancy shopping in that city, having worked out a bus and train route that took them through all the dullest backwood landscape, so they wouldn't enjoy themselves. Only, one spring they got fooled, for it rained and rained and the creeks and branches overflowed and they were detoured and passed through marshy woods full of dogwood trees in full bloom, lacy white, like something ghostly amidst the cypress and Spanish moss. They saw Judas trees flaming in the pale spring sunlight, under a blue sky harboring a flotilla of brisk white clouds. And climax of climaxes, they passed through La Grange and on the road near that town they saw the famous old cowcumber magnolia in full bloom, extravagant and towering. The old Yaupon Springs Hotel where they passed the night had a pianola and they listened enraptured to jumpy renditions of the *Moonlight Sonata* and *Pony Girls, Gallop Away*. You know where all this led: Atlanta was soon removed from their map.

"Soon," sighed Belladair, "we'll have to enter a monastery."

"I wonder," replied Mary Cross, "if that's really what you mean."

So at last all roads were closed and they stayed forever in Mobile, and visited their friends in the suburbs: at Isle aux Oies, on Dog River, at Spring Hill, and across the Bay. They were sitting on the pier of the Alba Club one day, an allegory of any two deities on any promontory jutting into any blue water under a cobalt sky, when their cousin Mrs. Henry Fifield brought her little grandson to leave in their care while she went to fetch crabs down at the Bridge.

"Will he be good?" asked Belladair suspiciously. "Or must we pitch him overboard?"

"Oh, he'll be good, won't you, hon?" said Mrs. Fifield, turning to Bartie, the boy.

"Mmmmmmmmmm," replied Bartie, staring at Mary Cross's wooden beads.

"Oh, well," said Mary Cross.

But as soon as the grandmother had gone off, after kissing the child, Belladair turned to Mary Cross and said in a low voice, "Sister, what do alligators eat?"

"Corporeal Corruption, sister, one would think you'd been born stupid—people, of course!"

"Oh, Mary Cross!"

"And a few dogs, I reckon. They love dogs. When a dog is in swimming, alligators in the bayous a mile away will come scooting, just clanking their teeth to get him."

"How do they know the dogs are there?"

"They smell 'em."

"How can they smell under water?"

"Well, sister, you ask *them*!"

"Not likely."

"Oh, they like watermelon rinds, too, I forgot that. They really like watermelon rinds."

"Well, Mary Cross, what do alligators *really* eat? They don't get people or dogs every day, nor watermelon rinds either, for the perfectly good reason that in winter neither people nor dogs go swimming, only lunatics like Fresh-Air Charlie; nor do they throw watermelon rinds overboard when they are not in season. Defies logic. If I asked you what do people eat, you'd say chicken and black-eyed peas, but I betcha there are people don't eat either, never even smelt 'em."

"Inconceivable."

All this time the child, forgotten, had grown more silent and motionless and now was edging his way under a wooden bench.

"Well," suddenly cried Belladair in a furious good humor, all giggles, "alligators would rather eat little-old bad boys than a gallon of ice cream."

Mary Cross glared: she was not given to frightening children.

"What they really like, Belladair, is well-seasoned spinster meat, and I'd as soon push you off this wharf as pinch you." And she pinched Belladair's leg hard. Belladair spat a mouthful of persimmon seeds at her sister, but they missed and clattered on the wharf, some fell through the cracks and splashed below.

They neither one knew of course that they'd entered Bartie's life with a crash of thunder and become his favorite dragons in two minutes flat. All summer he was left in their care, and if not, he trailed after them at a respectful distance, delighted to be faintly chilled by their conversation despite the blazing sun, and never drawing a sign of simple recognition nor a confidence from the two ladies. They adored to impose and terrify but never realized the gamut of love, and never knew how they had confronted Bartie on that ultra rim where fear and love are mingled.

Years passed in grand and stately tempo, with visits and gossips, until one October when they returned to town from a month at Dog River. As they came into the musty house (they always moved as quietly as shadows) they *felt* a presence, and tiptoed into the back parlor and there was a young man with black ringlets, in beat-up rather seafaring clothes, stretched out fast asleep on the sacred moss-green sofa where their papa had napped after lunch all his life. They both gazed and came all over prickles, stood there clutching one another like plum trees in a storm, till Mary Cross drew Belladair out into the hall, whispering instructions. Belladair ran across the street to telephone and the police arrived in no time at all. They stormed into the house, a whole posse of them, and seized the young man roughly, just as he was waking up. The Tollivers were delighted to have a real live criminal trapped in their house and studied him closely. He was young and had an open-air color about him. He only smiled, and never for a moment quailed or fought, even when the police grabbed him and pulled him about till his shirt was torn off. When they were dragging him down the steps to clap him in the Black Maria and haul him off to the hoosegow, Miss Mary Cross spoke up from her high front gallery (standing next to her forty-year-old Boston fern that was descended from one belonging to Augusta Evans Wilson, the celebrated author of *St. Elmo*) and she said, "If you please, I'd just like to ask that young man what he was looking for in our house."

"Money," he replied right away. "Because not only am I hungry, but I have a yen to travel to Fort Deposit and see my folks there."

At which both sisters laughed, but Belladair said, "Dint you have your breakfast?"

"No, ma'am, I haven't touched no victuals save a cantaloupe and some saltine crackers for nigh-on two days now."

Belladair blinked at that and whispered into Mary Cross's ear. Mary Cross thundered out, her voice carrying a block, "Well, officers, you better just fetch that young man back in this house, for I intend to feed him before he goes to jail."

"Miss Tolliver, you can't do that," groaned one of the cops. "Besides, we feed our prisoners."

"Nonsense!" snapped Miss Mary Cross, "the whole wide weary world knows that all you give the pore fools you got locked up down there is navy beans and cornbread made out of sawdust—*bring that boy in this house*!"

Whereupon Belladair piped up and yelled in her squeaky voice, "Our mother was a Wingate, and we will not have a growing boy going to jail hungry. Besides, it's Sunday."

Well, this growing boy was thirty if he was a day, but he flashed them a toothy grin, and the old ladies giggled—so what can you do?—the whole police and fire departments are as nothing before the delicate gold-wire wills of such as Miss Belladair and Miss Mary Cross; they had their way.

Once in the house they ran around like spinning mice preparing a real banquet for their favorite housebreaker; while he, in turn, stuffed it down, and turned in a plate wiped clean and paid them the compliment of a sigh or so and two or three expressive belches. These rough masculine signs of genuine enjoyment pleased their ladylike hearts and they ended making him have a bath, and giving him one of their late papa's shirts to wear.

"He might as well set out neat and clean for your ole roachtrap," Mary Cross told the policeman who had been detailed to stay and guard the robber. The policeman became the villain of the piece immediately, you see, and while the robber dined, attended by his two hectic Hebes, they all three would cast mute but pointed glances at the cop sitting out on the back porch sniffing the air wistfully. In the course of the afternoon he developed some small uneasiness and a large appetite.

When the time came for him to set out for the jail house in spite of all their delaying tactics, they decided to go too, and were so delighted to ride in the Black Maria they never even noticed Bartie, now thirteen and serious, watching wide-eyed from the corner of their yard. But ride they did and bailed out the housebreaker after he was docketed. He thanked them sweetly, and gave them both pecks on the cheeks, so they bought him a ticket on the L & N and sent him home to Fort Deposit. Even when they came back home and realized he had stolen the kitchen money out the Calumet can where they kept it, they weren't annoyed. They were only a little sad as they sat in the parlor sipping their cokes, gazing out the window to watch the yellow butterflies that come when summer ends.

When they discussed it at length they reluctantly realized they could never go out and about again: now they were confined to their own yard. The triumphant ride across the town to the jail house had been a Major Pleasure.

After that they never left their own yard, had the groceries sent from the corner store. Time went peacefully for two or three years then those three years came when there was no frost on the Gulf Coast, and summer went right on with three or four or more sessions of blooming. Plants they didn't know they had, or that had been neglected since their father's time, sprang up and blossomed frantically. A Vilma Vine that Professor Steele the naturalist had sent their mother climbed up to the second floor gallery and threw golden flowers all over the place. One old stringy thing in the front yard surprised them plenty when it grew up and bloomed and was a ginger plant. They had had it sitting there doing absolutely nothing for at least forty years. But the flowers! Soon as they cut them they came crowding out again, and those sisters got real silly over it after a while.

"So *tired* of zinnias, especially Lilliputians," moaned Belladair. "Tired of looking into their silly little old faces."

"Think about snow, just think about snow, that's what I'm doing," said Mary Cross with eyes squinched tightly shut. "I'm thinking about snow."

"Snow in Mobile?"

"Well, that's what I'm thinking about."

"Well, I'm not. I'm thinking of St. Brigetina whose martyrdom was she was smothered in flowers, that's what *I'm* thinking about."

You can guess the results: they went indoors and they never came out any more. They just stayed indoors, making handicrafts or giggling and looking at themselves in the mirrors. They'd make things like dresser scarves of linen with a design in red and brown floss of a windmill in the center and around the border what *may* have been tulips and what may have been a single-line marching party of drugstore beetles. The important thing is, those scarves are indestructible and lots of families in Mobile have them yet.

Then for a while their house was opened during the Azalea Season as a showplace for tourists, and when it was swept and dusted by the ladies of the Garden Club, it proved a charming image of the past. Mary Cross and Belladair at first hid in their rooms, but they soon began to enjoy hob-nobbing with the gawking visitors who poured through their parlors while a taffy-haired girl droned out a history of the old house while peeling off her fingernail polish. Being by now short of funds, Belladair and Mary Cross hit upon a wonderful way of raising money. In the dining room was a bronze chandelier from France, circa 1840, very Louis Philippe, all clambering metal convolvuli with tendrils and leaves. At the top was a kind of little cup around the chain that held the fixture to the ceiling.

"Betcha can't spin a quarter into that gold cup," Mary Cross would say, ignoring visitors.

"Bet I can," Belladair would retort, pulling a coin from her pocket. She'd try and miss every time. Then Mary Cross would try and fail. Soon, naturally, all the males would offer in gallantry to show them how it was done. They collected as high as $3.75 in one day from that cup, pulling the stepladder from the butler's pantry every day at six when the tourists were locked out. Later, they were forced to sell their furniture and the tours ended. They sold the silver and crystal next, finally the window draperies.

One day as they sat in their almost empty parlor, Mary Cross, who had been staring at the ceiling, suddenly gave a start and said to Belladair, "Tell me the truth!"

"What truth? The truth about what?" quavered Belladair, her pink mouth trembling.

"About everything!" cried Mary Cross, seizing her sister's shoulder. "About us! About just one thing!"

"What?"

"About Papa—did you *really* like him?"

Belladair's mouth fell open and for a long instant she stared in Mary Cross's blazing eyes. Then she replied in a low voice, "No, the truth is, I didn't." So they looked at each other for a long space of time, then burst out laughing. How they laughed, rocking back and forth, their feet stamping the ground, their hands clasped together.

Bartie, now Bart, now grown and home from the army, bony, but not underweight, having passed repeatedly by the Tolliver house, at last saw a sign of life. The door slowly opened. He stared hard, wrinkling his brow in concentration—he hoped to learn something.

Here they came: Mary Cross opened the door; she was 82 with short spikey hair, and a shapeless tweed costume given distinction by a fur piece of colorless spikey fur which so blended with her own hair that from behind, by moonlight, one would have said a tomcat sat on a cotton bale. She carried a velvet reticule, a paper shopping bag, and dirty white gloves. She left the door ajar and stood on the top step, sullenly kicking oak leaves off the porch. Belladair, at 80, was still a little reticent, making her appearance only after Mary Cross had cast a glance up and down the street. Then Belladair stepped from the shadowed doorway as from some lost dimension, as a luna moth leaves its cocoon. No light ever penetrated their shuttered pile, so she stood for a moment dazzled by the sunlight, poised and blinking, moving her arms meaninglessly, emanating—so it seemed—a dusty light.

Her hair was dyed jetty black, and on it she wore a huge Leghorn straw to protect her complexion—a needless apprehension since the most torrid of tropic suns could never penetrate the whiteness of her face, white with seventy years of studied pallor, white with such applications of rice powder that rice powder probably flowed in her veins with the blood commonly supposed blue but which more factually was a ruddy crimson fired with an excruciating and unbelievable passion for life. Her eyes were the color of amber; were set in superb bony sockets from between which a lost dessicated prow of a nose pointed to distance. The nostrils and mouth were young: tiny, tender, rosy, and childlike.

Belladair at 80 was still the tender maiden, delicate and upright; while Mary Cross, at 82, was a slightly stooped version of the same. Actually their faces might have seemed twin, save that twenty years earlier Mary Cross had given up rice powder and similar blandishments and now presented a mottled tan facade to the world.

Belladair daintily moved two steps forward and with a pointed toe kicked a leaf down the steps. Mary Cross stepped down one step. Bart, watching, shivered. Then the sisters stared at the world. No leaf crackled, no locust sang, no breeze stirred, the air was still, the sun was still, sounds of traffic from the center of town were miraculously stilled. It seemed they now would show their life's accomplishment: how they'd learned to hold time in their grasp.

Bart was transfixed. This mystery of arrest was the spectacle he had awaited. The moment was like a soap bubble still affixed to the pipe, still growing, alive, peacock colors swirling on a fragile curve. Oh crazy sisters! he thought. Although they were motionless, he knew in his heart they were galloping and that if anyone such as he remarked their full gallop and unswerving path, that they'd cry out together like ingenues that life was running away with them with the intent to pitch them into a convenient ditch, crack their genteel skulls and run off whinnying. But they moved not one hair. They had arrested Time and were staring hard into the obelisk face, returning hate for hate. The sisters stood there, and Bart felt that when they moved again, and he breathed, that trees would flare into bloom, seeds split the crust of earth, and accumulated sound come crashing about his ears, for they were holding the world dead still and when they let it go things would hurry to catch up.

The moment burst—Mary Cross slowly turned her head, and looked at Belladair who moved only her eyes. She held out the shopping bag and Belladair took it. Then they descended the stairs.

"Careful, sister, look what that oak tree's done," said Belladair where the sidewalk was buckled by the oak roots under it.

"I mind it, thank you," replied Mary Cross with the dignity of a small nation thanking a larger for the gift of an ugly statue.

The Tolliver sisters were beginning all over again from the beginning.

Beginning a new epic, a new faring-forth, had sighted a new planet. They both were Ceres and Persephone and both in the space of this fine summer morning would be ravished away to the Underworld. Both would weep and search, both, in two hours' time, spend a long season underground and return home in time for lunch. They were in the world again.

Bart, still in a trance, knew he had seen what he wanted to see: mystery, the unmeasurable, the commonplace strangled and skinned. He had come to question the oracle and it had replied, saying *life.*

He smiled slowly to himself, relieved to find all he remembered not only intact but amplified.

"I hope we can find some good okra," he heard one of them say, as they tottered up St. Anthony Street. Then he came to himself, knew he was free from them for good and and all, and went off the other way whistling.

The Charmer

Joel Trumleigh had what, for most American males, is considered a disastrous affliction. He was born in the Deep South of gifted and handsome parents who both died in an influenza epidemic when he was still in the cradle. Whereupon he was sent to be raised by relations, cousins, in the North. If he'd been raised in the South his affliction might have been less remarked, and he might have suffered less for it, but his formative years were spent close to that Rock on which set foot many of the ills which beset our nation: an unseemly fondness for the idea of a vengeful God, a fear of brightly colored pleasures, and a religious attitude toward money, as well as the idea that prayer is a form of fire insurance. Later, the cousins inherited a house near Montgomery and returned home to the South, taking Joel with them. But Joel was already in trouble.

And the trouble with Joel was, that he was an exceedingly beautiful young man.

The cousins who raised him adored the young man, naturally. One of them, Alice, was a World War I bride-widow, who had spent a lot of time in France in the 1920s. The other, older, sister, Charlotte, was shy, a musician, unmarried, scornful of men.

"There's a man for you," she'd say when little Joel tramped

mud into the back hall. Or: "Air this room out! It smells like boy!"

"Joel, who do you love?" Alice would ask.

"Black Beauty," came always his gruff reply. His first passion was horses and books about horses.

Alice couldn't hold her tongue. "But *you're* Black Beauty!" she would cry, and enrage the boy. But Alice was fun, and gave him his way, where Charlotte was a disciplinarian. Who could really resist him? He had straight slick black hair, red lips, and those green-grey eyes which corroborate an origin back there somewhere ago in County Clare.

His schoolteachers, mostly old maids when he was in primary and elementary school, never scolded him, and respected a gift of cold logic which early manifested itself in the young man.

But there were problems. There were fights and bloody noses: boys who had called him "Pretty Boy" or said "Pretty as a girl" or who said "Joel is a girl dressed up as a boy" or "Joel wears lipstick." It baffled Joel, who was a sturdy boy willing to play baseball until dark, or scale the tallest tree or highest wall. His face was always grave, unsmiling, and very beautiful, but he had the usual rusty knees, muddy shoes, and generally a rip or a tear. It was the face that no one could forgive in him, at the same time that no one could deny him anything.

When he was old enough to take girls out, it was the same problem. The first "date" was fine, but then the girl quickly saw that no one, male or female, noticed her at all: all eyes went quickly or dazedly or furtively or angrily or appreciatively at Joel.

When he was about 14 he was sent by Alice and Charlotte to a boys' camp for the summer. This meant a lot to him: he learned the pleasure of canoeing all alone on a vast mirror lake, and exploring, all alone, through woods or over hills.

Until one of the counsellors, a theological student of 24, began to follow him about like a pathetic hound, gazing enraptured at the freshness and calm of Joel's countenance. Every time Joel turned and scowled at him, the counsellor swallowed painfully, but he never stopped dogging the footsteps of his idol. It ruined the summer for Joel.

Back home he began to be interested in mathematics and began to devote a lot of time to study. He was bright, and had a natural curiosity. He won a medal at the moment of graduation from high school. He was happier than he had ever been, until after the graduation ceremonies, when everybody was going about swearing they'd come back to visit the teachers next fall, he overheard the mathematics professor in conversation with Miss Mingo who taught Latin.

"Joel did very well," he was saying.

"He's a bright boy," answered Miss Mingo. "But even if he wasn't, he would have gotten the medal. You've had him in class; you know what I mean. He could charm the paper off the wall."

The professor chuckled. "I suppose you're right."

"Every time I looked at him, I had to hold on to my desk. And when he got up to recite, all the little girls simply swooned. Swooned. He could charm the paper off the wall."

"Good thing," mused the professor, "that we are blessed with simple plaster and whitewash, then."

Joel took the medal home and put it in a box with his father's cuff links and never took it out again.

He decided he would like to learn music, and asked Charlotte to teach him. She had just turned 50, and was nervous. She started him out and things went fine—although she hid in her room with cotton in her ears when he was doing scales—until the day he turned to her to ask about some chord or other, and absentmindedly tapped her on the thigh. She had hysterics and never could explain why to him. Lessons ceased.

Then there arrived in town a minor Italian novelist brought to be writer-in-residence at the local university. Mr. Melchiori was 45 but looked older, had great shadows under the eyes and a generally gloomy countenance. His wife was plump, busy, and very efficient in dealing with their three children.

There was a cocktail party to welcome Mr. Melchiori and his plump Camilla. Joel and Alice were invited. When he saw Joel, Mr. Melchiori cried out, "Who is that piece of beauty?" which caused the good housewife next to him to choke on her cupcake.

"That's Joel Trumleigh," she snapped back, and unable to say anything she fell back on the local cliché. "He could charm the wallpaper off the walls."

"He has obviously visited the house assigned to the writer-in-residence," laughed Mr. Melchiori, "for I have remarked several sagging roses and one long strip of border hanging down very sadly." He left the lady and went to be introduced to Joel and his aunt.

"Che bellezza!" said Mr. Melchiori, smiling sadly to himself in gentle Mediterranean regret for summers and roses that were. "Do you know who Antinoüs was?"

"There's a photograph of his statue in my Latin book," said Joel guardedly.

"Come here," said the Italian to his wife across the room. "I want you to meet Antinoüs, only not as petulant, nor so soft."

Camilla, when she came, opened her eyes wide and stared long at Joel before she shook herself slightly and remembered to smile.

The lady with the cupcake, still with icing stuck to her palate, darted to the chaplain's wife.

"Dorothy," she muttered. "I think Mr. Melchiori is *queer.*"

"Oh," said Dorothy, unruffled. "No, dear, he's just Italian. They're always a little . . . well, I mean they're not as . . .

you see, the Mediterranean . . . no, he's just . . . well . . . broadminded . . . that's what a writer should be, don't you think?"

"I have growing boys," the cupcake lady growled.

"Oh, *boys*! . . . they'll do anything!" said Dorothy. "Besides, who isn't attracted to Joel Trumleigh? He could charm the wallpaper off the walls."

"That's just what I said!" cried the other triumphantly, icing now unstuck.

When Mr. Melchiori was leaving he went to Joel and patted his cheek, and closed his eyes for one instant in appreciation of the youth's extraordinary presence. Joel turned scarlet, not with embarrassment but with rage. He had begun to resent being stared at, being approached by strangers. He dreamed of living in a cabin in remotest Canada, with only some dogs and a caribou.

Later he became friends with Mr. Melchiori who was a perceptive man and saw the problem of being born so beautiful in a guarded world. Mr. Melchiori urged Joel to consider studies in Paris or in Rome. He often spoke of the Latin attitudes toward personal beauty—and toward youth and pleasure.

"I know I'm goodlooking," said Joel. "My mirror doesn't lie, and I have two eyes in my head. But I don't understand why people get so upset when they look at me."

"Some day you will," Mr. Melchiori said. "You see . . . well, for one thing, bold beauty doesn't go with the Christian humility that we are taught . . . but we Italians are not exactly Christians, you know . . . it's why we breed for beauty rather than for—what is your word?—utility!"

"Besides," Joel mused, "I think real beauty is a flashing experience, like when you solve a problem in mathematics —or the feeling in the air when the sun goes down on a very hot day: afterwards for a moment you feel the earth expanding and actually *smell* night coming. Beauty can't be an object or a person. It's an experience that lasts only for a flash."

"What about the great works of art," asked Mr. Melchiori gently, "that continue to give pleasure through several generations?"

"I've thought about that," said Joel briskly. "It may be youth and ignorance, but I think beauty exists for the artist just when he's put down the brush or the chisel and realizes that he did capture what he set out to. For the ordinary person it exists the first time he sees the work of art and gets that flash of perception."

"I see two things," said Mr. Melchiori. "One is that you are an earnest young man. The other is that the word 'beauty' does not come easily to young lips. Why should it? The word itself comes into English from Latin by way of Old French."

"Oh, I've heard about those old French," smiled Joel shyly, indicating that though he might be solitary and stern in his beauty, he did have some knowledge of the world and would be willing to speak man to man of follies.

"Joel . . ." murmured Mr. Melchiori, but then couldn't look at the young man when Joel turned to him. "When I was 17 years old . . . in Rome . . ." He thought better of it, laughed and said, "Come on home and have coffee with me."

Camilla served them black Italian coffee and *amoretti.* Camilla read English, but had difficulty speaking it. She took time out for lessons every day. She was genuinely fond of Joel, but inadvertently spoiled the Melchioris' friendship for the young man. She had heard the oft-repeated catchphrase and when she grasped its meaning, she sprang it over coffee.

"Ah," she teased him, beaming. "It is re-ally true what zay say: you can to charm the wallpaper off of the walls." This time Joel turned quite pale, and his visits became less frequent.

Joel fell in love. Like this: Alice had an old school friend, whose niece from Wilmington came visiting and met Joel as a matter of course. Her name was Emily; she was not really pretty, but she was more than that, she was all intelligence, and crazy-mad, her sense of humor was zany, she'd do anything to rile parents and authority. She had a delightful pointed face with ceaseless brown eyes. She had a tiny waist and wrists slim as reeds. Joel took one look and lost his famous calm. Anguish possessed him: he loved her, he loved her. She was a bird, a monkey, a toy to carry off and keep forever. They had a famous flirtation, sitting in the porch swing drinking rum and Coca-Cola and talking of absolutely nothing.

He took her dancing to a nightclub on the edge of town, a wild place full of students and soldiers from a nearby base. A jazz combo blared away, and when they rested, a jukebox took up the burden. Beer flowed like ditch water.

At a given moment a drunken lieutenant cut in on them, making Joel scowl. The lieutenant said—he was blond, clean-shaven, and milk-fed—"You are both too much. You don't belong here! You're a menace to us all." And he gave them each a fulsome kiss, planting it on their startled faces before they knew what was happening. Fortunately his friends got him out quickly, before the fight began. Joel swung but the lieutenant had already been lifted bodily out of harm's way. But the evening was spoiled.

The next day, Joel went to see Emily. Alice and Emily's aunt were there, having a drink and a gossip at the other end of the porch. Emily was very cool. Joel finally said, "I'm sorry for what happened, but what can I do? I wish I could have killed him."

"No, you can't help it," replied Emily thoughtfully, pursing her lips. "You are just born too beautiful to be on this earth. But you spoil things for everybody. He would have kissed me if I'd been a sheep dog with bear grease in my whiskers. That drunk kissed me because I was with you.

But he really didn't see me. He only saw that face of yours. I don't think I want to see you again. You scare me."

Whereupon Joel recoiled as if struck. He loved the girl, and already imagined their life together, although he had not yet proposed to her.

He went into the parlor where the bar wagon stood, and slowly poured himself a stiff drink, the color draining from his face. Then he walked to the middle of the room and stood there, looking about, bemused.

Emily regretted her sharpness although not her opinions. She went to ask pardon, but was stopped on the threshold by what she saw.

Joel was very slowly turning about, arms outstretched. He looked at the four walls in turn. They bore American Beauty roses on a chalky ground. He turned around again. The paper detached itself with great ripping sounds and moved towards him in jagged hulking sheets. Pictures crashed to the floor.

"What on earth?" cried Emily's aunt, and she and Alice started down the porch.

Now the silver and white paper on the ceiling collapsed in a rush and brought plaster dust with it. The chandeliers rattled and clanged. Joel was being wrapped in a paper embrace: tighter, ever tighter. Then the striped paper from the dining room whisked in, and down the stairs came great torn sheets of flowers from the bedroom walls. They lashed themselves about the figure of Joel, and as the aunt and Alice joined Emily and looked in, aghast, the odd bundled figure crashed to the ground. They saw the spasm as the last breath departed. Joel had done precisely what they had always claimed he could do.

Years later, when the fuss was over, everybody agreed that it was certainly the most original suicide of the century. There were some who breathed a sigh of relief.

Careless Willadell

The afternoon was still as dream, and Willadell thought the air was heavy on her arms, for all the world like a warm liquid, a tepid lake through which she moved with great effort, although she moved only her arms, carrying the sponge from the shoe-whiting bottle to the shoe she held in her hand. The chalky mixture had left bone-white driblets on her hands and on the back steps where she sat, and amused by these Willadell had thrown huge gobbets of shoe whiting on the elephant-ear leaves beside the steps. She giggled, thinking they looked like seagull droppings.

"Pretty big seagull at that," she laughed to herself.

"Still doing those shoes?" came her mother's voice through the shutters closed against the heat. Willadell frowned in irritation and said nothing, but waited with shoe poised in air for her mother's next statement.

"I said, still doing those shoes?" her mother's voice came again through the shutters. Then her mother turned over on the cot where she napped and there was a rusty *spang*! Willadell put the sponge to the bottle and shook vigorously and angrily.

"Oh, well," mumbled her mother, and sighed.

Willadell finished the shoe and put it next to the other one already drying. She put the sponge back in the bottle and screwed the cap. She looked at her chalk-caked hands, and leaned back against the top step. She squinted her eyes and studied the burningly green garden through her lashes. The pecan trees, the mimosas—all were still and brilliant. She watched some gnats around the trash pile that was already surrounded by melon vines sprung up from watermelon leavings dumped there two nights ago. She thought she could smell the heavy sweetness of rotting melon rinds and coffee grounds.

She yawned helplessly. Summertime, summertime. She closed her eyes in order to study the reverse image inside the lids—burning rose-red trees and a dark sky. What was it like to be cold, she asked herself, would she ever again be so? So hot and so drowsy, so—when she opened her eyes again she saw herself at the end of the garden, dressed in the pink and white Edwardian dress Eloise Logan had worn for Senior Class play. It was made of curtain material and she had itched to wear it herself, instead of the black costume she had worn in the maid's part.

"Lady Modesta regrets that she is indisposed and must forego the pleasure of visitors today," she said through clenched teeth, remembering the sticky make-up and the hot lights. But it was herself, she, Willadell, strolling in the end of the garden by the scuppernong arbor. She watched herself, fascinated but not particularly surprised. It was a dream, no, a movie; no, a movie of a dream. Or something.

Suddenly her eye, becoming a camera eye, swooped into mid-air, and she saw pass beneath her the trash pile, the tomato patch, the ruined trellis, the lawn mower abandoned earlier in the day by her brother. Willadell was in flight, moving down upon her own self—Willadell—strolling strolling strolling in Eloise Logan's Senior Play costume, carrying Eloise Logan's grandmother's parasol that Eloise Logan used in the play. As she came slowly to earth after an exhilarating parabola of flight, she saw the sunshade with hideous clarity. The bone handle, the ravelling silk braid and tassels, the sleezy cracked silk that barely hid the spidery iron ribs, the rust stains where the silk was attached to the frame. She saw herself raise the parasol with dramatic airs and graces, shielding her face which tipped coquettishly to one side under the tiny sunshade. Then Willadell moved toward her own face as toward a close-up on the movie screen, much magnified, in soft focus under the parasol, her lips parted, and her eyes half closed.

She moved still closer to the gargantuan countenance, staring at the mammoth black lashes, thick as cable, which opened and closed with the slow struggle of the luna moth, still sticky from the cocoon, essaying its wings. Willadell found herself moving nearer still, till she saw only two huge eyes, grainy like the movie screen seen from the first row. Closer still, and she cried out—or did she only think she cried out? —as she flew into one of the huge eyes, straight into the pupil, and heard the lashes close behind her with exactly the same sound as the iron gates of the Convent of Visitation. She was in black darkness for an instant, then found herself in a cypress swamp, which she guessed was Chickasabogue. She was leaping from hummock to hummock, holding onto boughs to keep her balance, and clutched at by an infinity of twigs and branches. Something was chasing her, she vaguely knew.

She looked down and realized that now she was no longer spectator, she was performer. She saw her feet shod in the pointed white satin slippers Eloise Logan had worn, pattering out from under the pink and white ruffles of Eloise's dress. She sniffed and smelt the faint salty glue-like smell of the sizing that is in curtain material before it's washed. She was fascinated by her own two little white satin feet, miraculously spotless in the midst of Chickasabogue Swamp. She watched how when one went forward, the other disappeared beneath the ruffles, then suddenly the hidden one leaped forward and planted itself firmly on a hummock of moss. Her slippers were gleaming, lustrous white, and she realized that color had gone, she was living a black-and-white movie in some crazy way.

She murmured but no words came. Now she heard the background music throbbing and whining as she clutched a pine bough and wondered if she would faint and sink into the black mud. Twilight had come suddenly she thought, but looked up and realized it was only rolling gray clouds, synchronized with the music, and speeded up a little, it seemed to her. How they tumbled, and faded, how the light pierced them, then mingled with them as they curled and foamed over. As much like water as clouds they were, busy and full of contrary motions. She longed to sport amongst them, aerial and carefree, but realized the power of flight had left her. Then as the music swelled to a shrill tingling climax, she heard a terrific thundering snort, and a faint burst of air whipped her ruffles against her body. She was naked under her dress.

She looked down and saw an alligator fixing her with his beady eye, not six feet from her. She gasped, and clung to her pine tree. The alligator slowly opened its mouth, and with a great thrill of pleasure she saw the rows of white teeth and the rosy flesh of his tongue and mouth. Now I'll surely faint, she thought, but instead found herself calm and sharply observant. She bent over and took off one shoe, which now was so brightly fluorescent that she realized her shoes were emanating light of themselves. She looked at it an instant, then smiled cruelly before she tossed it into the alligator's mouth. His jaws too, she remarked with wry interest, closed with a metallic clang like the convent gates. At the moment that he swallowed her shoe, her head swam, and she realized she had become spectator again, and there before her was herself again, in sharp black and white, silhouetted against the burning white sun which made her dark hair gleam. But BANG! and the world turned negative, and she saw her hair, suddenly dazzling white and silken, thrown out as in slow motion, flayed out around her head and obliterating the black sun in the sky.

Oh, now it's like underwater, she thought, and later remembered thinking it. But colors came back just then and she heard a kettledrum rolling. She saw herself flee through the trees, now knee-deep in water. Every time she put her shod foot down, the satin shoe hissed when it touched water. The branches switched her and tore off her dress till only the two sleeves were left on her, and otherwise she was naked. She stopped to pant, but the alligator lumbered up out the black water beside the tree where she stood. This time she saw herself carefully remove the remaining shoe, and slowly stretch her naked body along his scaled and ridgy back, her head above his head. Then she reached out before his jaws and proffered the shoe, which he snapped from her hand, and crunched happily. Snow began to fall, and suddenly she saw her own image grow enormous and sink down into white mud like blanched caramel. Then the music reached such a crescendo that she felt her rib cage shake, and she coughed and coughed and put her hand to her mouth and coughed up a tiny white sugar shoe, smaller than the smallest sugar lump.

"It'll stick in your th'oat, chile," she heard her old nurse Jennie say, who had been dead for four years.

It's only on the soundtrack, they have an old recording of her voice, Willadell told herself in a superior and knowing fashion, just as a flash of light blinded her for an instant, and the green world returned. She was at the end of the garden, looking toward the dozing house, and saw herself again, as she had been on the steps, dozing in the hot sun, clutching one white shoe to her and fretfully turning from side to side on the hard steps. Then the air rushed past her as she regained her sleeping body and she woke with a start, disgusted. She threw the shoe down the steps, and it rattled going down. Her mother woke.

"Willadell, what's that?" But Willadell said nothing.

"Willadell?" Her mother's voice was sharper now, she was waking up, and soon they'd have cokes on the back porch.

"Hmmmmmm?"

"You still doing those shoes?"

"No'm."

"What are you doing? What was that noise?"

"Nothing."

"Oh, humbug, it must of been, 'cause it woke me up." But Willadell picked up the polish bottle and, taking careful aim, smashed it against the brick wall. Before her mother could ask, she said, "Oh horrors! I've dropped the polish."

"Honestly, can't you be more careful?" said her mother, irritated.

"No!" shouted Willadell flippantly, but after all, quite honestly.

In The Orchard

When they stepped from Beauford's car and slammed the doors, the sound frightened some bluejays who flew into a pecan tree and sat there talking against the intruders in an irritated manner. But not for long. The day was too fine to admit any outcry or complaint—a blue sky harbored some puffy clouds and the silliest of breezes bearing the smell of the salt sea—so after a moment the jays flew down again to the tangled thicket of Cherokee rose and blackberry that had claimed the fence, even in places obliterated it.

The visitors were three: a young girl with a merry pointed face, dressed in a plain cotton frock and expensive white gloves; a pale woman of fortyish with black eyes, dressed as though to represent Anonymous; and a tall leonine boy whose shaggy black hair had once been described as a fit home for elves and dormice. He tenderly held a battered leather journal, in a manner suggesting the all-night reader and true bibliophile.

They stared at the house—huge, ramshackle, encrusted with alcoves and balconies, garnished with jigsaw fantasies and half covered with wisteria and coral vine. The edifice had a tenuous and uncertain air, seemed to contemplate the possibility of soaring into flight like a crazy flying ship, if it could be disentangled of its burdens of greenery. Looped and curled in space like a primer of the baroque, the coral vine burned with color. The house hinted at having once been painted a dashing yellow, but now showed green age and gray-weathered wood.

"Like a stage setting!" said Miss Mennin.

"Mmm . . . " mused Imogen, smiling.

"Looks deserted, or dead," added Beauford.

They stood as if magicked, in spite of the breeze dousing them with freshness to encourage movement, even dance.

"Do you think she's here?" asked Imogen.

"Oh, she must be," answered Beauford.

"Let's don't stay too long; I'm hungry," said Miss Mennin in her mild voice.

"Me too," agreed Imogen. "It's the air." She had torn off her gloves and was plopping blackberries in her mouth, purpling her lips.

"Well, stop stealing from the jaybirds and come on," growled Beauford, and opened the gate, setting up a great clanking and ringing from the cowbell and bits of hardware fastened to the gatespring. They stepped into the overgrown yard, knee-high with fringy grasses and field flowers. A cast iron ibis mooning amidst some cast iron arrowleaves showed where once a fountain had played, long since dry and full of leaves.

"Ruellia," commented Miss Mennin, pointing at small blue flowers, "kind of country cousin of the acanthus."

"Another world," smiled Imogen, "just another world."

"Here comes *somebody*," shrilled Miss Mennin. A proud negro man was coming around the corner of the house. Only his rheumy eyes and a certain delicacy in placing his foot revealed his exceptional age.

"How-do," he said with a courtly smile.

"How d'ya do," they all murmured. Then Beauford spoke: "We've come hoping to see Mrs. Carly de Banfield. I hope she's home."

"Oh yes," the old man replied. "She's to home. She never take herself out anymore a-tall. Miz Carly set herself to read all the books in the world."

"Well!" laughed Imogen meaningfully as a jibe at Beauford's well-known bibliomania, "I can certainly see that'd keep her from socializing. But we won't take her time. We just want to speak to her for a few minutes."

"Why, shore, shore," the old man said. "She back here, and she-ull be tickled to see yawl," and he motioned them to follow. They did so, were brought under a crumbling porte-cochere, past many tall windows, to a half-wild pear orchard behind the house. Under the fat pillowy clumps of foliage hung with sand-colored pears, the black trunks seemed to march drunkenly on to infinity. Hedges and shrubberies edged the wild orchard, shutting away the outer world.

In the center of this richness sat the Sibyl herself at a rustic table made of tree boughs, creaking now with the weight of books and tablets arranged as though disarranged. Yes, Mrs. Carly de Banfield as ever was, ageless in lilac-swiss flounces and stringless tennis shoes, chip-diamonds in her ears. On her head, perhaps aping Minerva's helmet, was insecurely piled a great dome of white hair, stuck with tortoise hairpins. Deep in a book, she seemed not to hear, then looked up suddenly and fixed them with a stare, closed the book ponderously as if it were the Book of Life and she had just erased a dozen names. Laughter had etched on her face a complex map of joy, furrows and gullies to drain off hastily any sorrow which might appear in her brown eyes.

But what delayed the polite greeting of her guests was the fineness of her honey-colored skin which revealed no great age, though they knew she had passed seventy; and the fact that on her upper lip she sported a delicate white mustache, maybe twenty or so white hairs brilliantly distinct against her tanned face.

Surrounding her, almost humanly attentive, were chairs: beat-up kitchen chairs, Victorian wicker rockers, weathered dining-room chairs, even a rusted metal-tubing *moderne* number, hopelessly out of place here.

"Never see a Bearded Lady?" she demanded delightedly of their silence, then in a gracious gesture indicated the chairs. "Please sit down."

"Mrs. de Banfield . . . " began Beauford.

"Mrs. Carly sounds better," she interrupted.

"Yes'm . . . Well, I'm Beauford Branwell . . . I think you know my father . . . "

"Know you too," she broke in. "Knew you when you were an awful bad little ole boy at Miss Minnie Duval's."

"And who are these young ladies?" she demanded of Beauford before he could catch his breath.

"This is Miss Mennin and Miss Runciman."

"Mennin? Mennin? I don't think that's an Alabama name."

"Oh no, I'm from West Virginia."

"But *you*, you must be one of Nannie Lee Moten's girls. I remember when she married Alex Runciman. Better, I remember the engagement party. I was there. *Everybody* was there. And more lighted candles than you could shake a stick at. Oh, it was beautiful. Which sister are you?"

"She's told me about it; it must have been. Well, I'm Imogen."

"You have two sisters, and one is named for my good friend, Miss Ninetta Fifield, whose name suggests stuttering. What's the other?"

"Named Annaliese, for Mama."

"That's right. I forgot. Imogen, Netta, and Annaliese—well, she could have done worse. Thank God, no Mary this or Mary that. I swear I would have sent you home. I loathe the commonplace."

"What was your name," asked Beauford, "before you

married Mr. Carl de Banfield?"

"Not common, but not expecially pretty either: Lettice Hannaford. As a child I yearned for Reba and Charlotte, but after Maeterlinck appeared I thought only of Mélisande and Monna Vanna."

"L.H.! L.H.!" cried Imogen to Beauford. "Mrs. Carly is L.H. in the Journal!"

His eyes lit up. "Of course! The Journal is *before* she married Mr. de Banfield."

"Poor old Carly," mused the old lady. "I sometimes forget what his face was like and have to totter into the parlor to the picture album. Though of course it's Lettice who died, too, and I am a living amalgam, a ghost of the happy pair. My mustache proves it."

"Mrs. Carly, we have a question to ask you," began Beauford.

"Ha, ha, you're going to ask why I don't shave it off," she laughed.

"L.H. was married at Bladen Springs," Miss Mennin reminded her companions, which set off questions rattling like strings of firecrackers in Imogen's mind and Beauford's, but Mrs. Carly kept on.

"Ah . . . Bladen Springs . . . of *course* poor pretty dumb L.H. was married there. Confederate jessamine everywhere, people call it star jessamine now, there're always fools in the world, yes ma'am! Oh, and fiddlers, a fluteplayer from Demopolis, and tables laid out with rich rich rich rich food, ham in a thousand ways, a thousand kinds of devilled eggs, wine cooled in the springs, and punch bowls scooped out of watermelons and edged with scuppernong leaves. Oh, the world *needs* parties, and always will!"

"Did you know anyone there whose initials were N.D.?" asked Imogen.

"Doubtless! But I had more than initials. You should have

seen my *drawers!* I found some in the attic a month ago. I can't tell you their most prepossessing feature, but over the left knee of each pair, above the eyeletting, was my name in white cotton—white on white—spelt out in a delicate lady-like italic."

They all smiled, then Imogen put in quickly: "Do you happen to remember a May Day party at Bladen Springs where some young girl from Citronelle was crowned May Queen, and somebody recited verses for the ceremony? We'd love to know who recited the verses. You see, we have this Journal kept by somebody who was there, and . . . "

"Oh, everybody made verses in those days. One had to either ride well or make good verses. Or simply be beautiful, whether male or female. One of these three was expected. You should see my scrapbooks."

"I thought you'd remember, maybe . . . "

"Fiddlesticks! I remember Carly's youth and childhood better than my own, 'cause when he died I went back and lived his life over."

"I gathered . . . " began Beauford.

"Rosebuds while you may, I hope. Not ideas, they should never be in bundles, that's for field peas. Ideas should be separate and shiny, like ripe plums. By gathered I hope you don't mean you construed. Jolly Jesus! Strew rosebuds, after you've gathered them, but *con*strue nothing; never assume, never take upon yourself, never conject. To construe is to send for ducks when swans are needed. Oh, life should never be construed, for then it can never bloom star-like around us, unexpected as rain lilies that pop up overnight in wet places. It's what I've learned; I've learned a great deal, I learn every day. It's a daily dose of disclosure keeps me alive, not food or drink, though of course with patience I worry my way through a little chicken and a glass of wine now and again.

"Oh, the outrageous mysteries that dance under out noses! A gavotte of elephants and gnats. But never construe . . .

"I used to judge people by their faces, their gait, eyes, hands, their accent, their clothes, their manners, above all their laughlines, smiles, laughter . . . but now I squinch my already squinchy eyes and measure them by their past and their future . . . a kind of borealis light that plays in the air around their heads . . . nimbus is a pretty word . . ."

"Aureole too," said Imogen, swept along in the Johnstown Flood of talk. Mrs. Carly pretended she heard "Oriole" and cried "My favorite bird!" and went right on:

"To construe is to categorize, and to do that is to accept mediocrity which I consider a besetting sin, like snobbery, which in turn ranks next to murder. But to murder mediocrity is a virtue, perverse as philosophy must be, and that's why I wear this mustache like a white pennoncel flapping in the breeze."

"It's not that long!" cried Miss Mennin, shocked by the image.

"Sweetie," intoned Mrs. Carly, her eyes closed and her eyebrows raised. "I like to think of myself as Vitus Bering sailing the sea which carries his name, discovering his first walrus, who returning the glance thinks *he's* discovered his first mirror: I mean, a *walrus* mustache, which I'll have yet.

"If I were much younger I'd wear elegant black men's clothing, with dapper tight breeches and a pleated shirt. And wickedly pointed black patent leather shoes. Maybe even smoke a cheroot. This I'd do to give proper ladies a turn, but also because since I was fourteen I've wanted to cut a caper in men's clothes. Oh, I could be a Wild Girl! You probably think I'm crazy, but dear loves all, thank God or whoever if this be so, for then I'll prove the most yellow-spangley Penny Poppy Show seen in these parts!"

She paused and took a deep breath, gazing past them into

the trees, but no one stirred save curls and wisps on her head tugged by the breeze.

"Up North," she went on meditatively, "madness is buried like a mandrake root and has to be dug up to either scream or sing while here, my dears, it just blossoms like the rose and sings like the june bug: the air its habitat. Healthy and thriving, thank you. Yes, we all are loony here, we live in sweet lunacy's county seat. That's why I've spent a lifetime carrying pencil and paper to prod Inspiration for a name at once incisive and obligatory, remote and musical, to call this property . . . and never yet have set it down. A vintage madness . . . oh, I could name you names, but you all know . . . but for a place-name what's it ever to be? *Noddinia* or *Feu-de-perle* or maybe *Nimbusand* (for my theories) or named for the poets: *Herrickell* or such. The loveliest word in the French tongue is *luciole*. Well. We'll see. Though of course it's really the seacoast of Illyria; 'And what should I do in Illyria, my brother he in Elysium!' Why, what I'm doing here, now. Burden the air!"

She laughed, delighted with herself and her opinions, then lit a cigarette which she drew from a cardboard box covered with braid and seashells. Imogen, noticing the vast pencil collection—stubby, eraserless—saw that the paint had been nibbled off where usually was printed Number One or Number Two.

"My attendant spirits, my maddies," she continued, pointing vaguely down the orchard, "and my masters of learning are down there. Soon you'll hear them. The mysteries are enacted there, Eleusinian and otherwise. I've learned all the secrets of life and art from them. Did you ever think . . . " she looked into the eyes of her guests in turn, "that a swarm of ten-year-old boys could prove such seers?"

She paused to skirmish among her books and papers, seizing a paperbound catalogue of sculptures from the Louvre and ruffling its pages.

"There!" she cried. "Look!"

They craned forward to study the picture indicated by her bony finger. It showed Eros sleeping, a slim beautiful boy of maybe fifteen years, wings half closed behind him, bow held languidly, one foot trailing off the embankment or hummock where he rested.

"I've known this all my life," she said firmly, "and loved it for a lovely thing in stone, but now for me it breathes air. Virgil, Theocritus, Herrick, Mozart have all come to me in the form of a swarm of little naked ten-year-old boys paddling in my creek! The inane lovely secrets are to be learned from them.

"Oh, such screaming and yelling, such whooping and hollering as you've never heard! Then I know they're there and I walk close to the hedge down to the end of the orchard where there is an old falling-down summerhouse. The last hurricane took the roof, but wisteria made a new one. I can go right in there and sit down, after I've assured myself there are no snakes. So I'm enthroned, with dirtdaubers and such pests to share my royal box. 'They tell me that the Lion and Lizard keep, etc.' Well, the spectacle is on. Such things as I've heard and such things as I've seen. You wouldn't believe! But I just sit there not knowing enough to laugh or cry.

"I have to be careful not to wear white or they'd see me. Therefore I am bright, solemn and vestal in my spirit; but all faded, patched, all worldly in my garb. Sometimes, even so, I think they know I'm there. You see, we are in love, they and me.

"That is, I do indeed love them, as one can love the Poets and have tears sting the eyes and hang in the lashes over the beauty of those lines that leap from the page. And if necessity or fatal need is a kind of love when its face is washed and its hair slicked down, then they love me. They need always to know I am in my orchard. I am a kind of mustached Ulrica and my house, of course, is haunted.

"Oh, and we're such fakes. They come marauding in this orchard stealing pears, frisking in the trees loud and sassy as jaybirds. Then I pull myself up tall, carrying a rough stick, waiting till twilight if possible, and hoping I seem a veritable Gorgon against my big ole house. If I have not seen them enter, they conjure me by crying imprecations or throwing pears on that metal-seat chair. I show myself, fierce and unsmiling, yet inwardly so full of tenderness I think I may light up like a jack-o-lantern. I move slowly down the orchard, the while they invent new insults and throw pears. They pretend to mock me, but their respect is infinite. Many a time I've slipped up back of one of them and seen him turn white and drop his booty when he realized I was there. Once I couldn't come outside for laughing: they all sat in a tree, yelling 'Mrs. Carly is a bootlegger!' at the top of their lungs, their sweet insult for that day. So tell me, how can you explain any of this at all, save to say it's a love affair?

"You see, you see . . . " she coughed and nodded her head. After her long outburst, neither Beauford nor Miss Mennin looked up from whatever they stared at, charmed to silence. But Imogen shook herself and sat up very straight and said, "Mrs. Carly, we have an old Journal here with some fine poems in it; we thought you might tell us the author, since you're mentioned."

"Why," asked Mrs. Carly, "didn't you say so? I could have looked at it first thing, if we hadn't been talking so much."

Imogen took the battered volume and put it in the old lady's hands. She opened the cover, and at that instant cries were heard down among the trees.

"Listen! Listen!" shouted Mrs. Carly, banging the table for silence, though no one spoke. She narrowed her eyes, staring against the light at the row of trees. But it was jaybirds crying, and she turned again to the book. While she studied the yellowed pages, a light wind crossed the tops of the fruit trees and shuffled all the leaves.

"Oh, yes," she said with a slow smile. "Yes, indeed. I know very well who wrote all this, but I won't tell; that is to say, I may not—no, not ever. You see, once I was performer . . . but now I'm custodian . . . "

The Kewpie Doll

Mississippi, 1939

Dawson had seen enough funerals. First, that of his beloved little grandmother, who had raised him. Then that of the guardian, *in loco parentis*, to whom he'd been consigned by his grandmother's will. The last rites for a school friend drowned at Point Clear. Then a great-aunt. Then his dog Michael. Then his cat Tommy. So the summer he graduated from high school, he ran away and joined the Reforestation Camp, under Army auspices, in Mississippi.

Already regretting his act, he sat in the back of a pick-up truck bumping over the oyster shell road, along with six other adolescent boys bound for the same camp. He knew already that he was the outsider, for they were all being sent from reform schools and were all illiterate. But they did all share a coating of white oyster shell dust, hair stiff and on end. They looked like the *Living Statues* act in the Ringling Brothers Circus.

Dawson had never known "country" folk before, since Mobile is basically Catholic, Frenchified in the last analysis, and certainly fun-loving. The puritan Anglo-Saxon strains of up-country Alabama were exotic to him and its language almost incomprehensible.

"I dar ya to call me 'Tater-Nose' one mo' ass-bleedin' time," a pudgy short red-faced boy was saying to a tall skinny red-haired youth. "Iffen you do, I'll make *yo* nose look justalike that toad-frog that took on the Greyhound bus from Laurel."

But soon it was twilight and they had arrived at the camp.

"Hell," said the Sergeant who checked them in, "yawl look like a passel of ass-bleedin' ghosts. Git in there and wash that white crap off, 'cause supper is ready, then we gonna break yawl in on night duty."

To Dawson's horror, that first night duty turned out to be a wake. One of the boys in the camp, one 'Lijah, had died in an epileptic fit, strangled on his own tongue, out in the woods where the boys were planting trees. No one had known how to save him.

"My God," thought Dawson, "how did I let myself in for this." He looked around at the green-grey benches, the green-grey walls bare of any ornamentation whatever, nor clock nor calendar, the plain pine coffin resting on two sawhorses. Two of his fellow recruits were playing mumblety-peg, the *thwacks* of their knife blades into the soft pine floor the only sound save the buzzing of insects around the bare light bulb. Dawson felt lost, infinitely sad, a sadness which almost buzzed like an insect somewhere in his rib cage.

With the first light the Sergeant came to relieve them, and then all the boys in camp were herded in for a funeral oration by an effeminate, lisping, pink-fat preacher from up the road.

"Some folks think death is only a form of refinishing . . ." Dawson heard him begin.

The next day the newcomers were interviewed, questioned, looked over by the Captain and Major who ran the camp for the Army. They were prodded, poked, fingerprinted, made to feel hopeless. When it came out that Dawson had studied painting and drawing Major Tratt shook his purple jowls and said, "Ah-ha! Then you could paint sign-boa'ds, cuncha?"

"I reckon," replied Dawson.

There was an open-front shed behind the army officers' quarters. Here were big unpainted wooden rectangles intended for road signs, their eventual supporting posts leaning in a corner. Shelves of enamels and brushes.

"Here you be, Painty," said the Sergeant, having already rechristened Dawson. Everybody in the camp had names other than their own: Red-on-the-Head-Like-a-Peckerwood, Hitler, Crawly, Bentwood, Lard Ass, Big Un, Little Un, Pokey-Pisser, Miss Meow and so forth. Dawson accepted "Painty" without argument. The Sergeant found an official book giving measurements and colors for the official highway signs and left Dawson to go to work.

"Too good to be true," thought Dawson, as he opened a tin of flat white to start giving ground-coats to the signs.

"Lawd, Painty, you got the soft-ass job, dint ya?" said Big Un, passing by to fetch his shovel. "Who you suckin' up to?"

"Happened," shrugged Dawson, carefully laying out brush strokes.

When they all went off in trucks to plant trees or to fight forest fires, only the administrative clerks and the kitchen crew were left in camp. Dawson quickly got into his own routine of working hard the first hour, then propping up the official manual and drawing pictures or writing poetry behind it. He could see or hear anybody approaching on the gravel outside.

Or so he thought. But one day, when he'd finished the orange-red lettering on a BRIDGE OUT sign and had begun on a huge SOFT SHOULDERS for the new highway, Dawson looked up and saw a wizened, unsmiling, young but old-looking man squatting outside the paint shed, making a great to-do of *not* looking inside. The man reached into his shirt pocket, pulled out his packet of *Bull Durham*, then some tan paper, rolled himself a cigarette with long-practiced dexterity, reached for matches and lit up, threw the matchstick over his shoulder, replaced the matches, took a long draw, studied the gravel before him, all this time still squatting. Suddenly he looked up, frowned, and squinted at Dawson.

"Hey," he said.

"Hey, yourself," replied Dawson softly, in the manner of the district. But he was thinking, "Now I have met Mr. Pellagra in person. Owes his soul to the company store, no doubt. . . "

"You Painty?" asked the man.

"Thas how they calls me," said Dawson, still affecting the local manner.

"You paint them signs?" asked the man, making an inconclusive gesture toward the big slabs of wood.

"Yeah," said Dawson.

"Well. . . " the man hesitated.

"Yes?"

"See. . . I thought as how maybe you mighten cud paint sumpin' for me."

"What is it?" asked Dawson, beginning to be puzzled.

"Well. . . my baby chile done died off in the night. I made her a nice little ole coffin. . . I thought maybe as how you mighten cud mark her name on it. . . "

The man rose slowly to his feet, went to some bushes nearby, and drew out of them a small unpainted pine coffin. Without a word he brought it inside, placed it on Dawson's table, opened it and revealed a greenish, waxy little corpse, doll-like, too small, almost, to be human, lying on a scrap of flowered cretonne. Dawson's guts winced at the sight of the tiny fingers curled on the tiny hands. The man closed the coffin wordlessly and waited for Dawson to speak.

"Sure," said Dawson, nodding, with a stiff throat.

After a moment he added, "Shouldn't I paint this thing white before I put her name on it?"

"Iffen you take a mind. . . " said the man.

Dawson painted the coffin white, then went back to his signs while it dried. The man squatted just outside the shed, smoking and watching the ground, teasing some ants. Even the usually nagging Sergeant said nothing when he came by; he got the picture. After a few hours the white paint was dry on the coffin and Dawson lettered the infant's name on the lid—CLARY HOBSON—and painted a simple wreath of green leaves around it. The man had come back in and watched as if hypnotized, especially during the lettering.

"Is that her name?" he asked.

"Yeah."

"What kinda leaves is them?"

"Oh, myrtle, I reckon," said Dawson, out of the blue. The man opened his eyes wide for an instant.

"Myrtle?"

"Yeah."

"Thas. . . " stammered the man, "thas my wife's name, Myrtle. . . " He stared, fascinated, at Dawson. "What do you want? I ain't got no money, but I can bring you a pullet . . . or a duck."

"Nothing," replied Dawson. "The paint is Uncle Sam's and I'm willing to oblige."

"I'm mighty beholden," said the man, still wide-eyed, then hurried off into the twilight, the coffin on his shoulder.

But the taciturn Mr. Pellagra must have opened his heart to the local grapevine system, for a host of suppliants turned up in subsequent days.

Just three days later, a bedraggled gray-faced woman of no age at all turned up with the lid of a larger coffin, for, say, a ten-year-old. She paced in boldly, put down her rifle, placed the lid on Dawson's paint table and whispered, "Jim Trout . . . in a circlet, like you do." And she went and squatted outside. Those were her only words. But she rewarded Dawson with a brief grave smile when she hauled the lid away.

Thus it began . . . every other day a baby coffin to paint, usually for the newborn, or young infants, some from as far away as Carroll County, once even from Corinth, Miss. Once a special coffin for an "old man" of around fifty years. His two sons, with eyes brown as chinquepins, full of life (did they keep pigs and were well-nourished?) brought some wrinkled First World War army papers and wanted the long registration number, as well as a Probate Court registration number, copied on the lid. The younger, more solemn son asked Dawson to "limn out an aigle" and Dawson didn't understand, and they went on and Dawson finally understood they wanted an American eagle.

Death . . . thought Dawson . . . I'm caught up with Death . . . my life is all coffins, funerals, all death. I shall die too, how can I not, with every day a feast of death, a pageant of coffins.

Major Tratt himself looked in one bitter cold day when Dawson had just finished lettering JIM HORN on a lid painted blue as had been requested.

"Shi-itt," said the Major. "Ain't very cheersome in heah, now is it? Nothing but disasters." He gestured with his huge beef-slab hand. "You got your BRIDGE OUT, you got your NEW ASPHALT, you got your SOFT SHOULDERS (we'll talk 'bout that tereckly, ha!) and then to keep cheerful, you got all them goddamn unlucky shit boxes. I tell you, Painty, iffen I was doin' yo' job, I'd turn into a gloom-ass for sure. . ."

"Sir, I tell you the truth," said Dawson, "I am most likely turnin' into a gloom-ass."

So shortly thereafter it was ordered by the Major that

Dawson should work a two-hour stint as personal orderly to him. He was to make the Major's bed in the mornings, take out ashes, wash last night's whiskey glasses, sweep out the quarters. Dawson was pleased by these orders, since the February days in that open-front shed were blastingly cold, the weather as depressing as the coffins. Dawson had lost weight, become quiet and moody.

"Ball ache," was the general diagnosis among his companions.

"I wonder," he mused, "if they'd faint should I tell them what it is I suffer—soul ache, would they know that malady?"

He was sick of the eternal horseplay of his companions, of the cold, of the dreary barracks, the ghastly food, the dead grass, the cold . . . most of all, the coffins.

So he went with a lightened heart to do orderly duty in the officers' quarters. The yellow pine walls and floors were cheering, and the place was deliciously warm.

He went to work with a will. When he'd made the bed and carried out the ashes from the fireplaces, laid new fires, he seized the broom and swept vigorously. The Major had told him he might play the radio, so he swept in time to *Flat-Foot Floojie with a Floy Joy* and *Love Bug'll Get Ya If You Don' Watch Out.* And, as he swept, he suddenly heard a strange buzzing or clicking sound; he stopped to listen, then the sound ceased.

"Deathwatch beetles," he thought. "Will I survive my seventeenth year and live out my eighteenth?"

He heard it again the next day, and turned off the radio to trace it. But nothing. Nothing.

One day he discovered the source of the sound. It came, muffled, from inside the clothes closet. He opened the door cautiously. The sound stopped. He moved aside a military overcoat, some trousers hanging from clip bars.

Then he saw her.

A Kewpie Doll, about eighteen inches high. Gawking, he brought this object out into the room. Outside the gray rain fell straight down, a dark day. He turned on the bedside lamp, placed the doll on the trunk beside the bed.

He knelt on the floor to study her. Suddenly, with the clicking and buzzing sound he'd been hearing before, her big wild eyes began to roll, her hips to gyrate obscenely. Her hula skirt of yellow silk lamp fringe tossed seductively. Her hands, plaster, were fixed over her head where every marcelled curl had been neatly painted in thin lines of gold over the same corn yellow as her skirt. Dawson watched wide-eyed as her hips swayed and ground, a dusty music box mechanism plinking away some unrecognizable tune. Dawson stared. She glittered. Her fingernails were gold.

He lifted her skirt.

Where her sexual organ should be was the dial of a clock, with phosphorescent hands.

He turned the Kewpie Doll around, noting her huge painted spit curl, her painted shoulder straps of tight yellow rosebuds.

On her enamelled buttocks were the knobs and the button to set the alarm.

Slowly, he began to comprehend her functions. If one set the alarm properly, the bell would ring at the prescribed time, and the Kewpie would begin her gyrations, which continued until she ran down or one pressed the alarm button and turned her off. Obviously the Major often forgot to turn her off. Did he retire her, hide her every morning? Back into the closet with you, my dear. . .

Dawson stared at her a long time.

Then he went into the sitting room and poured himself a glass of rum, carefully putting enough water into the bottle to bring the level of the liquid back to what it had been before. He gathered all the *Esquires* in his arms and went back to the bedroom. He arranged the pillows, placed his glass at hand, then wound up the Kewpie Doll, set the alarm for *now,* and watched her begin her dance, her eyes dizzying over her painted smile. Her eyes rolled, her fringe flipped. Dawson drank, lying against the pillows . . . shoving off his shoes . . . loosening his belt. . .

"Honey," he said, in the local style, "the first time I heard you, you scared me so much my ass was cutting buttonholes. . . "

He watched her wild hip-slingings.

"Jesus," he said, "but it's nice to have a friend when you're away from home." He lifted his glass. "I'm drinking to you, Rough-Stuff, here's mud in your goony ole eye!"

She went *click-grind, grind-click,* dancing.

He laughed.

The Back-Roads

I always laugh when people complain of Sophia County being staid, or boring, or a too comfy-cosy family sort of thing. Some communities *are*, I suppose, and small towns the world over are pretty dreary affairs, after all, if you're stuck in one. But Sophia County's not dull, heavens no. It's only trouble is that it's up-country, inland, instead of on the Bay. Well, and there are all those Greek farmers not far off, and that Yankee factory going up fifty miles away, where they'll manufacture electric can openers.

I'm going to tell you a story and you can decide the moral yourself.

Well, my cat there, that you admired so—he *is* an unusual color, isn't he? Few cats are that red. Look how he's looking at us with those big yellow moons. I love the way his paws curl up under him on the cushion. You know, in the fall when my chrysanthemums are in bloom, he can stalk through the bushes and not be noticed, he matches those reddish bronze flowers so. Funny, I never was a cat lover before. Never owned a pet before him. No, not even as a child.

My husband and I had no children. But ours was a happy marriage, even though we both were somewhat sad at being childless. But we had a fine garden, we travelled, we read together—all kind of books; we read every night in winter, and drank mulled wine.

When Phil died it was in those books that I found him again. I read over all the things we'd read together: I'd hear his voice in every line. Even so, after his death I felt almost as if I had died too. I felt . . . well, *submerged.* I mean, you know, out of touch with the world. And people were so nice, and I hate sympathy. I simply had to go about things in my own way. Can you understand?

People were so *nice* to me that I withdrew from clubs and committees and just stayed at home. Sometimes the car stayed in the garage for days at a time. Finally I even lost interest in the garden. One day I was putting up strings for the sweet peas when I realized I didn't care one way or another if they had strings to climb or not. So they ran all over the place, like wild, and full of dead flowers, since I didn't bother to pick them. People began to say, "Poor Laura, how she's changed since Phil died," and that just riled me and I let the garden go completely at last.

Well, so two years passed like flat nothing or like two centuries—both. On the second anniversary of Phil's death I pulled myself together and decided to go over to Linden Bridge where he's buried in the family plot, and put flowers on his grave. So I poked around and filled a basket with late asters and chrysanthemums and collected my gardening things and set out.

I set out after lunch, about two o'clock, I guess, around then. It was a sunny day but with a few clouds, and the leaves were just starting to have a tinge of gold in them. I arrived at Linden Bridge about three and set to work weeding and clipping and setting out the flowers I'd brought. His brothers never bothered to do more than put an evergreen wreath once a year, so there was a lot of work to be done. After about two and a half hours I'd put things to rights. I found it most refreshing, tugging at the weeds, and enjoyed the sour green smell of the peppergrass roots I'd pulled and piled in a neat pile. When I'd finished I sat on the corner of Phil's father's stone and smoked a cigarette and enjoyed the utter quiet of that country graveyard. I watched the Spanish moss swaying, swaying, in the two live oaks by the gate. I was in a kind of spell when I left, peaceful, thinking placidly of the peacefulness of the tomb and of all the generations which had passed this way since the Spaniards landed in 1519.

The shadows were long and the yellow light dusty when I started back—and somehow turned wrong, in my reverie. I didn't notice, even, until I heard a furious honking back of me. In the rear-view mirror I could see a huge black Cadillac driven by a chauffeur and contrary movements of three or four dark figures behind, urging him to pass me. Before there was time to pull half off the road to let them pass, I noticed, with a start, that I was lost, in a part of Sophia County I'd never seen or had I strayed into Baldwin County? There was a line of sand pears along the road, low rolling hills—could have been anywhere in the world. The sky had clouded over too and the changed light added to my sense of estrangement. I glimpsed, across the meadow I was passing, a furtive gleam of water under a clump of trees that had already gathered night about them, even before night had come. Where could I have turned off? How had I ridden into this unknown country? The Cadillac was already far ahead, churning up a cloud of whitish dust.

I stepped on the gas, determined to overtake the Cadillac and see who was in it, but more than that, wanting to stay by it, since it was the only sign of life in that dream-like countryside into which I had somehow wandered.

The stillness of evening had claimed the world and the bushes along the road were ominously still, full of gathering shadow, but washed across their tops by a last greenish-yellow light that escaped from under a lid of gray clouds that pressed down the sky, save for a rim around the horizon. Far ahead I saw the Cadillac taillight illuminated just before it made a turn to the right. I bumped and joggled madly ahead on the rutted road, panicky now. But I found myself, when I turned, too, on a paved highway unknown to me, and like the other road, deserted. There was a filling station with three people sitting before it. I passed a signboard and my heart skipped a beat as it was illuminated just at the moment I reached it. All I saw was the motto, "For Beauty's sake . . . " What, for Beauty's sake, I asked myself, biting my lip. Well, love, death, and folly was my reply. On I sped, forcing my old wreck of a car to overtake the black dot ahead that was the vanishing Cadillac. I still had no idea where I might be.

But I did find myself overtaking that slick black car. It had stopped to let a truckload of gravel ponderously cross the highway from a gravel pit to one side. Just as I came close, the Cadillac purred and started on. But it's a cinch now, I thought, as I followed.

My eyes went, as any driver's will, to the license plate, which I noted, again with a quiver of nervousness, was covered with a neat black waterproof cover of some sort, therefore told nothing.

Inside the car, three women—I assumed them to be women, by their dark clothes and the shawls or scarves on their heads—were bobbing their heads, and gesturing wildly—laughing, arguing?—as we sped through silent woods and fields. I saw they were tossing something about.

Suddenly my growing sense of mystery and terror deepened when I saw an object tossed from the window of the speeding car and realised that what had been ejected by a long black-sleeved arm was a live kitten. I slammed on the brakes and jumped from my car. With tears jumping suddenly to my eyes, I ran blindly along the road, looking down at the shallow ditch. I found the kitten at once by his marvelous russet color. He had landed in a low bush covered with convolvuli and was suspended in the vines, all four feet spread out, his eyes enormous. He was dazed but seemingly unhurt.

"Baby, baby," I said soothingly as I put out my hand, glad I was wearing my driving gloves in case he'd be terrified and claw me.

But the kitten simply looked at me and uttered the most plaintive long-drawn cry you've ever heard. I gingerly extracted him from the vines and stroked his fur as I carried him back to my car. He was trembling. I examined his legs ever so gently but he was quite unhurt. I suddenly was overcome with fury at the unknown women in the limousine, so, placing the kitten on my folded apron in the gardening basket next to me I prepared again to overtake the Cadillac.

As I stepped on the gas and shot off, surprising myself by the fury of my speed, and the elation of my anger, another car passed, the first I'd seen, and very reassuring.

Then the sun peered out of the clouds just at the horizon and sent an orange light across the road.

I saw that there was a village ahead and that the Cadillac had slowed down. Fearless of traffic, of police, I plunged on and overtook the Cadillac just beyond the village as it was stopping for a red light at a crossroads. I jumped out and rushed to the side of it, blazing with anger. But what I saw robbed me of speech: three old nuns, their faces like wax drippings, watching me with bird-like fixity.

I felt I might faint. I thought—here you must bear with me and understand as clearly as possible what I want to say. I'm not a fantasist, but this is really the way it was. I thought that in the gloom I *might* see on the lap of the middle Sister the decapitated head of my father as a young man . . . or a mound of ice . . . or a dozen red kittens rolling together . . .

or I don't know what. What I saw actually were these three ancient Sisters and a great bundle of dead branches. I was speechless because ever since my childhood, in catechism class, where I never knew the lesson, I've been afraid of nuns. Odd how childhood obediences come back. Once I visited my niece's third-grade classroom and when the teacher rapped for order I trembled and was as much of a mouse as anyone there. But these ladies wore a habit I'd never seen. Were they visiting chanoinesses? Sisters of some other faith? Were they the Devil's saeter-girls disguised as nuns? I crossed myself without thinking, but as the motor of their car started up my anger returned full flood.

"Fiends!" I shouted, screaming so loudly I heard my echo from the woods alongside the road.

They all three laughed but no sound reached me through the heavy glass of the window. The Cadillac shot away and left me in the middle of the road feeling a fool, but more alive in every vein than I had been in the two years since my Phil died.

I went back to my car, which was boiling, and peered at the kitten. He was still exactly where I'd placed him in the basket. I took him in my arms and stroked him and he settled down at once, his eyes never leaving my face.

After my nerves had calmed down and heart stopped racing, I started up the car and went on down the highway until happily I found a filling station. As I filled the radiator I learned that I was not far from home after all. I had come a kind of long way round on a road I'd never known. (I must add that to this day I've never found the route again. I've gone up and down the highway but have never hit upon that little dusty turn-off where I first saw the Cadillac. I'm not sure I really want to find the road, you know.)

My first concern when I was home again was to carefully examine the kitten. I found him to be obviously well fed, with a lustrous coat of the remarkable color you see there now, only somewhat lighter then.

He had no aftereffects at all, save for a fear which he still has of people with a hood or kerchief on their heads. Otherwise he is magistral calm itself.

And how can I ever tell you, even for one small instant, what he has been to me in these years?

First of all, in the days after finding him I seemed to wake from a deep dream of grief—which had nothing to do with grief itself—and to live again. I studied my garden with a scandalized eye and set to work, weeding and pruning and planting. I opened the house to the autumn winds and banished tons of bric-a-brac to the attic. I painted. I had a new haircut.

And Barbarossa, as I named him, sat there, oh just as you see him now, with wise eyes and courtly manners, or walked the garden like a meditative cardinal. But he tosses field mice just as the nuns tossed him, to a great distance.

Wait a minute, there's the kettle, I'll make the tea.

And what does it all mean, you ask? Well, that mystery exists even in the back roads of Sophia County, and that behind or below the safe and cosy there is always another insistence which is dark. There are corridors that General Electric cannot light nor Grand Rapids furnish. There are days that fall outside recorded time, hours that amaze, happenings that have another light, another gravity.

We are too prone, I think, to name, to count, to take for granted. But life is a fire-cloud, not a rock, and rock itself is illusion. No, the demonic must be served, but most of all we must not forget to marvel. Or to seize the here and the now.

Forgive me, I'm not a philosopher, nor a preacher either. I've gone rambling on and the tea will be ink. Oh, you like it strong. Good.

But to finish, Barbarossa has been a symbol of all I can't explain, of all that cannot be explained to me. Look at his eyes. Did you ever see such?

I thought not.

Shall we ask him to join our tea party? He could have this cushion, and I'll give him cream.

Oh, watch him stretch. Come on, my little sir, here!

How many lumps do you take?

The Byzantine Riddle

On Mobile Bay, the late October afternoons are golden and still, long and summery.

The group of ladies had finished their tea under the pecan trees and had fallen into a cosy silence, watching ants going off through the grass struggling with crumbs of kumquat cake. They would have preferred some music, although no one thought of it or mentioned it. The silence remained oddly unbroken and at last began to weigh on them.

Mrs. Warden had the habit of lowering her voice when she had something to impart which she considered serious and worthy of total attention. She lowered it now, as far as it would go, so the other ladies recalled their shimmering minds and willingly gave her the floor, or rather, lawn.

She said: "The masculine sense of humor is basically very frivolous, very primitive and, above all, cruel."

"Oh, men never grow up," sighed Mrs. Cantwell, rubbing her eyes and sitting up straight.

"I *mean* . . ." said Mrs. Warden, coming back up to an easier conversational tone, "well, you just take what happened at Bessie de Banfield's last week. If my husband had behaved like that, to me, after all that happened, I swear I'd'a shot him."

"What did Tom do?" asked Mrs. Cantwell, mildly.

"What happened, what was all that that happened?" asked the old dressmaker, Miss Grenier, who hadn't been listening. But she pricked up her ears at Mrs. Warden's last words. Men she conceded, but husbands were her natural enemies. After all, they were slow to pay her neatly written bills and somehow didn't seem to notice her, tapeline about her shoulders, mouth full of pins, even in their very own houses.

Mrs. Warden turned to her. "Honey, where have you been? Up on some mousseline cloud?"

Miss Grenier almost blushed. "Well, I've been so busy . . ." She kicked a pecan leaf with a pointed white kid toe. "I sewed three thousand and four hundred bugle beads on Emily Baxter's train for the Leinkauf School coronation. It's a full time occupation. My eyes get too tired to read the papers."

"Oops!" whooped Mrs. Warden. "You'd never read about *this* in the papers. You mean you didn't hear about Bessie's party for the Modern Idea Club?"

"She founded it . . ." murmured Mrs. Cantwell, in a "there-there" tone.

"I wasn't there, I had those bugle beads . . ."

"Lord!" sighed Mrs. Cantwell. "Neither was I. Billy had fever. Wish I'd gone anyway."

"Tell me . . ." said Miss Grenier.

"Lord, yes!" chimed Mrs. Cantwell. "I could hear it over a dozen times. Cissie embroiders a new detail each time she tells it."

"Do *not*!" raged Mrs. Warden. "My memory flickers, that's all."

"Come on, hon, flicker for us now," begged Mrs. Cantwell.

Mrs. Warden only laughed. "I tell you what, ladies, let's stow away these tea things and fetch that bottle of Jim Beam which is sitting right on the icebox beckoning to us. I need a nip if I'm gonna do a number." They all giggled contentedly and rearranged the scene. Cups were whisked away and in no time ice tinkled in the long glasses.

Then came Mrs. Warden's voice in the prologue, down again to its lowest note.

"Well, Bessie de Banfield has this big party every year for the Modern Idea Club . . ."

"Which she founded and which she runs . . ." said Mrs. Cantwell lazily.

"Indeed. She thought we should put our minds on the problems of the day. Every week a different problem, then at Christmas and every Mardi Gras she gives a fun party, sometimes with a speaker."

"And always *her* idea of fun," put in Mrs. Cantwell softly.

"Her mother was the first Mobile lady to smoke publicly," explained Miss Grenier.

"She does come up with some clever ideas, that's the Lord's truth. It was her idea to make the friendship garden on Hall's Mill Road, and if she hadn't taken the initiative they never would have saved those stone squirrels on the roof of the D'Olive house. She led the march of tree lovers to City Hall that time . . ."

"I wasn't there . . ." said Miss Grenier.

"Cissie, you are going to get the details in the wrong order again," admonished Mrs. Cantwell. "Tell about the *dog* now."

"He doesn't come in yet."

"If you don't tell about him *now,*" said Mrs. Cantwell, "you'll ruin your story by having to slow down and explain about him when he does come in. Tell about the decorations and about the dog *before* you start the party."

"What dog is that?" asked Miss Grenier suspiciously.

Mrs. Warden closed her eyes patiently against interruptions, then dropped again to her thrilling contralto.

"Bessie de Banfield is not exactly what you'd call an animal lover. She has been known to bag cats that cross her property, to protect the birds, although between us the cardinals have not put foot one in her yard since she cut down those two tallowberry trees by the carriage house. Last year her feeder stations went untouched, save by squirrels, and they cost her five-ninety-five apiece F.O.B. Michigan."

"Cissie," said Mrs. Cantwell gently but firmly, urging her back onto the road.

"Anyway, you all know she's hot on astrology, and she read her forecast for the day—oh, about a year ago—and it said, 'An unexpected visitor today; be sure you make him welcome,' and then she went out in the yard and there was this little shaggy dog sitting in a lawn chair like he owned the place, sassy as you please, and waggin' up a gale. So she fed him, pried the cockleburrs out of his fur, and kept him."

"What kind of a dog?" said Miss Grenier.

"I'm telling you the story, honey," warned Mrs. Warden. "It was just a *dog* dog. It had one black eye, and one white, and was shaggy with a busy plumey tail. Very well behaved, but hated horses. Didn't chase cars. She tried to find out where he belonged but didn't. She got fond of him."

"Now, the decorations . . ." prompted Mrs. Cantwell in a stage whisper.

"Bessie it was who chose the club colors, and the club motto," quickly related Mrs. Warden. "She wanted the motto in Latin or something medieval but nobody could put it into any of those for her. The motto is 'Think up and out in every direction.' Tom de Banfield wrote out *'Faictes tout que voulx vouldrez'* as the translation, and lots of people had fun over that. The club colors are blue and gold and the symbol—don't ask me why—is an old astrolabe that belonged to her papa. She had it sketched to put on the club paper. One year she had a big old astrolabe made of wire and covered with flowers, which she put on the lawn for the party."

"Not this year," put in Mrs. Cantwell. "She just got some paint . . ."

Mrs. Warden overrode lustily: "Just got some paint and painted every stick of lawn furniture yellow for the party. Blue linen cushions and tea cloths. Bessie has yellow coreopsis all along her drive, don't you see, and the shady wall of her house is covered with blue plumbago. So everything *fitted in*, she made everything blue and yellow. Including Bessie herself: silk print."

"I made it," said Miss Grenier. "It was ochre and teal."

"Everything went together," continued Mrs. Warden. "*Everything*! She went to Three Georges and had mints made in blue and yellow. Then she went to Smith's Bakery and ordered cupcakes made in two ways: yellow ones with blue icing and blue ones with yellow icing. They said, 'Mrs. de Banfield, it's been our experience that folks won't touch blue cakes, it's just not an appetizing color,' but Bessie is like a battering ram when she takes a notion, so she got what she wanted. And more besides, which is part of my tale."

"She's biggety," sniffed Miss Grenier.

"So then she made two punches, one colored with blueberries and much too sweet. The other was golden yellow and it was made of peaches and muscatel. She had a blue mayonnaise with yellow egg salad, and a bright yellow mayonnaise with slices of breast of chicken colored blue."

"Sounds ghastly," said Mrs. Cantwell.

"Nobody touched the blue meat," said Mrs. Warden. "It just sat there looking disconsolate."

"Were the men there?" asked Miss Grenier.

"Well, you know, Tom gets them all out on the side porch with a bar wagon. They know by instinct when the ladies have been served and drift in afterwards to the buffet. But they were out there laughing. I think they tell dirty jokes. This year Bessie asked all the members proper to come an hour early so we could get up a note to send the Governor about the sterilization of criminals, which he proposed, and which was coming up for a vote in the State House the day after the party."

"There's another thing they can do with men like that," said Miss Grenier thoughtfully. "I heard about it."

"What do you mean, hon?" asked Mrs. Warden.

"Oh, yes, castrate," said Miss Grenier. "It may be something Fidel Castro invented. Anyway, you know, for criminals. Castrate them."

Mrs. Cantwell looked genuinely pained. "I hardly think . . ." she murmured, then turned gently to Miss Grenier. "We'll have a little talk when you come over to do my linen suit."

Mrs. Warden went right on. "We were for rehabilitation and sent off our telegram to the legislature and that was that.

"Then the party commenced. There were thousands of people and since the paint wasn't quite dry on the furniture most everybody stuck or at least had their clothes ruined. Nobody would eat that blue breast of chicken. There was heaps! Bessie is very old-fashioned about hospitality and believes there's got to be enough to have tons left over afterwards. Her servants have come to loathe chicken salad. Mélisande O'Rourke recited Amy Lowell's *Patterns,* then Elise de Feo played the *Ritual Dance of Fire* and *Girl with the Flaxen Hair.* They were having the dessert, including those blue cupcakes, when it started . . ."

"Tom de Banfield . . ." prompted Mrs. Cantwell.

". . . was not drunk, just flushed like he gets. All the men had come around by then and were having a big laugh over the blue food. Tom kept making jokes about ptomaine poisoning every time somebody bit into one of those cupcakes. They all laughed, but lots of them left cupcakes with just one bite out. In the midst of all that hoo-ha that little dog came running in and ran up to Bessie who was holding court in the patio. She broke off a piece of her cupcake and gave it to him . . . and ladies . . ." she paused for effect, looking at each lady in turn ". . . he just plain *dropped dead!*"

"Cissie!" they all cried, meaning "We don't believe a word of it, but tell the delicious horror again."

Now Mrs. Warden rose to her heights. They all felt she should have gone on the stage. She brushed imaginary crumbs off her lap with a languid punctuating gesture and slowly recited: "She gave him a piece of blue cupcake, is what I am telling you, and the poor little beast immediately *croaked.*"

"Oh!" They were impressed.

"She sat there looking at the dead dog, then at the bit of blue cupcake in her hand, then at everybody standing around, too staggered to say anything. So she called her husband."

" 'Tommy,' she said, 'is this animal *dead*?' So he bent down and had a look, then he said, very seriously, 'Yes, ma'am, with a blue cupcake *seething* in his jaws.' Well, that did it. When he said that—somehow Tom had already sabotaged the party with his ptomaine jokes—but when he said that, the first thing that happened—after a terrible long silence when nobody would look at each other—was that Mélisande O'Rourke threw up. It sounded like Niagara. Right on the flagstones!"

"Nervous girl, always was," commented Mrs. Cantwell.

"Whereupon all hell broke loose. Lots of less delicate and more practical souls just put their fingers down their throats and let fly, and I wish you might have seen Marie-Louise Fields, Elspeth Bradley, and Emmeline Bradley all bent over the lilypond like the Three Un-Graces!"

"I'm glad I wasn't there," murmured Miss Grenier. "It sounds plain horrible. Did it harm the goldfish?"

"I could die that I missed it," laughed Mrs. Cantwell, brushing tears of unalloyed pleasure from her eyes. "But after all, my papa was a doctor. I reckon I have another kind of sense of humor."

"What did the men do? What did you do?" asked Miss Grenier.

"We did the same, actually. Marched into the house and got ourselves big slugs of brandy. But that's only the beginning. You know how Bessie rises to an emergency. She took over like a field marshall, and had a fleet of ambulances and interns there in a flash. It was a scene of carnage, yes, a scene of carnage. Upstairs, all those ladies were laid end to end and had their stomachs pumped."

"I'm sure it did most of them a lot of good," roared Mrs. Cantwell, rub-a-dubbing her feet in merriment. "Especially that bridge luncheon set!"

"It was a scene of carnage," said Mrs. Warden. "Just a scene of carnage."

"Were you . . . pumped out?" enquired Miss Grenier, distastefully.

"You bet your sweet lolly I was not!" cried Mrs. Warden. "I knew not even a coral snake could kill that dog so quick. I saw that he *hadn't* eaten the piece of cupcake; it was under Bessie's chair. Afterwards . . . oh, three or four days afterwards, the newspaper boy told Bessie how he'd seen a truck hit the pore little dog. It had run to Bessie for help. Everybody was threatening suits, or to disband the club, so Bessie made that boy come before the meeting and tell what he'd seen. He was tongue-tied when he stood up in front of those ladies in their hats; she had to *prod* the story out of him. But he was one of those cotton-top up-country boys; everybody knew he wouldn't lie or make it up so Bessie was cleared."

"That poor little shaggy dog," sighed Mrs. Cantwell.

"Well, I don't know that I think Tom is so bad," said Miss Grenier thoughtfully. "If he really said 'seethed' when he examined that dead dog and referred to the cupcake, I feel it was a most precious and apt choice of word. I think it's . . . funny."

"That may very well be!" glowered Mrs. Warden, "but

that wasn't the worst. Late that night, when the victims had been dismissed and the premises mopped up, there was Bessie almost dead with fatigue and anxiety—she didn't collapse until the very end—and she was propped up in bed with her cold towel on her head and trying to take a little cognac, when here comes Tom in a funny plastic hat and carrying an ancient automobile tire pump he found in the garage. He strolled in, took a slug of her brandy, and pumped his pump a little—wheeze! wheeze! He says, 'Excuse me, madam, I represent the Wragg Swamp Stomach Pump Corporation. I'd like to tell you about our handy Party Plan.' "

"He didn't!"

"Oh, yes he did! She really broke down then, but now you'll see why I say the masculine sense of humor is cruel, cruel. Afterwards he walked up and down on the side porch outside her bedroom window and ate a whole plateful of blue cupcakes."

"He didn't!" the others cried.

"Not only that," intoned Mrs. Warden tragically. "He made loud smacking sounds as if he enjoyed them."

"No!" cried Mrs. Cantwell, but Miss Grenier stifled a burst of laughter, only the others let it pass for a snort of dismay.

Mrs. Warden held up her hand imperiously, and silence fell.

"The next morning," she said, "he walked into Bessie's room and smiled in the most *natural* way, and held out a plate and said, 'Have a cupcake!' "

Now the others were silent in disbelief.

"Oh, I don't know," said Miss Grenier shyly. "I've never been married, so I don't know. The masculine sense of humor has always been a Byzantine riddle to me. How do they think up the things they come out with?"

"Oh, hon," boomed Mrs. Warden frowning slightly. "Men don't *think*. They just laugh and scratch and say the first thing that occurs to them. Only women have second thoughts and even third, and decide which one to *use*. Besides, the dealings between men and women are full of Byzantine riddles."

"Gothic, too!" exclaimed Mrs. Cantwell, eyes sparkling with a saucy meaning she had no intention of sharing. Then, very seriously, she handed about an imaginary plate. "Have a cupcake," she said mildly.

At which they all hooted.

But Mrs. Warden quickly recovered herself and, very much in charge, held up an admonishing hand. "Enough! I've told you how it happened." She placed her empty glass on the table with a slow and beautiful gesture of antique finality.

Natural Habitat

Martin Hobbins was a sour man. A book reviewer who'd been at it too long, he had tossed off a great many book reviews, but he had never made an anthology, never written a book of essays on *The Blossoming of the Mid-West* or *After the Petulant Generation*, never served on a committee judging a prize-novel contest, had achieved notoriety and influence without quite knowing exactly why . . . and turned sour.

So—aging, and wrought-up—John Hobbins so far forgot himself as to write a very testy review of *Down in the Glyndon Marshes*, the latest *roman fleuve* from the Southern novelist Morgana Weston Hadley, who, as everybody who reads must know, is a first cousin of Henry Hadley Weston who edited the paper John Hobbins worked for. No time at all before the editor sent for him.

"I *know*, John," said the old man, beginning to cloud up. "But here where you refer to her 'antidiluvian' style, and this snide little remark about 'our semi-literate authoresses' . . . I mean, after all, goddam it, she *did* go to school in Europe. Besides, the book's not that bad. I read it. Morgana may not be the new McCullers, but she's not as meaningless as you make her. She tells a good story. I sat up to finish it." The old man tossed the clipping across the desk, then moodily watched it flutter to the floor.

"Tell me the God's truth," he said, "have you ever been down South?"

"No . . . I haven't," said John.

"Well . . . you've got a lot to learn. People *do* talk like that, and there *is* something baroque about it all, and they do have all the kinds of trees you object to in Morgana's book. Magnolia's a damn fine tree, just let me tell you. You oughta go see for yourself."

"I'd love to," said John, very sarcastically, only when he saw the purple rising in the old man's face, he hastily changed his own expression so it seemed he really meant it.

"I think we can arrange it," said the old man, fixing John with a bird-like stare.

Which is how John Hobbins found himself with his patient wife Sarah, and a pile of new books for review, chugging through the Deep South one fine day, heading for a tiny village in Alabama not far from the edge of Marengo County. In the absence of the authoress Morgana Weston Hadley (on a lecture tour of the Far West) he was to have a vacation in her house *Glynrose* ("Grisly" had been his private comment) in order, according to old Mr. Weston, "to learn about the South, calm your nerves, and eat a tee-toncey wedge of humble pie."

Sarah, although aware she should find the trip distasteful under the circumstances, was full of a glee she found difficult to conceal—she adored travel—and hummed as she watched the woods and fields fly past the train window. Once they passed a mule-drawn wagon full of cotton-headed country children, who all waved gaily at the train.

"Local color," said John gloomily. "Local color."

"Oh, why don't you break down," laughed Sarah, "and have a good time."

But now he was hearing the chattering of the train wheels, which seemed to sputter directly to him, "Dichotomy,

dichotomy, dichotomy, dichotomy," until he sighed and closed his eyes.

"I hate the South," he mumbled. "I hate extravagance and exuberance and all that lackadaisical sense of things, no form, no form . . . I wish . . . "

She didn't let him finish. "That's hardly the attitude with which to begin a vacation," she observed, then looked out at a tiny country station whizzing past.

"Oh, Charleyville! The next is us. Next stop is Palmyra Junction."

"Palmyra Junction," muttered John. "See what I mean?"

The village was seen, through the glossy pines and dusty chinaberry trees, to be small, hot, and lifeless, situated on a plain. Low green hills rose beyond, on whose thickly wooded flanks stood several large white houses. The arrival of the train was accomplished with scarcely any commotion: the stationmaster appeared at a leisurely gait, some freight was dropped off casually, a dog crossed the platform, changed his mind and crossed back, a few passengers descended and wandered off. John was vaguely annoyed at not being met when he saw a most charming creature picking her way delicately toward him. She was about seventeen, with pretty slim legs, barefoot, in shorts and a torn boy's shirt or a boy's torn shirt. Her flaxen hair straight about her ears. She came up to within seven feet of the new arrivals and looked at them boldly for a long instant. She smiled and said very slowly, "Hey." Then she turned and walked off.

Just then a man of about forty appeared on the dirt road by the train platform. He was hurrying along, carrying a pie on each upheld hand. The train blooped and pulled out, drowning out John's mumbled question to the man, so, annoyed, John had finally to shout over the train's noise.

"I said, can you please tell me . . . "

"We'll talk about it some other time," the man shouted

back, quite pleasantly. "Lime pies, you know." And he hurried on.

Sarah laughed, but John scowled, speechless. He picked up the suitcases and hurried across the platform toward the village. As they clonked down the wooden steps to the road they noticed that there was a booth on the shady side of the small station building. It had a huge Coca-Cola sign over it, and an assortment of magazines and paper-bound mysteries, along with candy bars and such. It was tended by a handsome black woman in a black and white silk dress, with starched apron and russet turban. She regarded them with interest as they approached.

"Excuse me," began John with an air of defeat, "but can you please direct me to *Glynrose*? You see . . . "

"Oh, everybody knows you're coming, Mr. Hobbins," said the woman with a smile. "I've been on the lookout for you. So has the president of the Women's Club. If you're not careful you're going to be killed with kindness."

Her accent, they both noticed, was quite cultivated, almost London.

"If you wait just a minute, I'll run you up to the house. My car's here and I'm just closing for the day. I only have to get out of my Dixieland drag. Oh, I'm Dorothy Shaw. I don't live here; my home is in Michigan. But I'm down here doing research for the Swedish Insitute of Sociological Studies, I have a grant. Sort of statistical supplement to Myrdal's work, you know. But not everybody knows that and that's why I'm done up as a Southern-fried mammy, and I'll thank you to keep my secret. Excuse me."

So she rattled the shutters of her booth shut and disappeared for an instant, reappearing in a chic beige suit dress, carrying an expensive looking briefcase.

"Now," she smiled, "I'm *me*. But let's get into the car; it'd never do for me to stand around town looking stylish. I have to wear that Mandy costume if I'm going to do business, and have to do business to get my facts. I had hell getting permission to have the booth anyway, and even then they wouldn't let me have it inside the station. Still . . . all this will mean my doctorate."

Recovering from their surprise at her quick change, John and Sarah began to pump Mrs. Shaw for facts on Palmyra Junction. Levelled by The Yankees in The War, they learned, restored and made to prosper at the turn of the century by the first industrial enterprises moving South, then ruined again when the railroad line was built about forty-five miles to the East instead of through the town, Palmyra Junction had settled down to its quiet county seat existence, enlivened by an occasional visit of Circuit Court or gospel show, and amused continually by the capers of its own and only celebrity, Morgana Weston Hadley.

As Mrs. Shaw's car drove through the main street, shopkeepers filed out onto the sidewalk in a dawdly manner to have a glimpse of the newcomers, the latest rare birds to arrive under Morgana's sponsorship. The man at the icehouse, busy wrestling a watermelon into place on the bumper of a truck, stopped in his tracks and waved.

"Well, howdy," he called, and Sarah smiled and nodded.

"Don't encourage them," scowled John, "after all, we *are* on a vacation."

"Don't worry," said Mrs. Shaw. "They won't bother you, they're really quite pleasant when you get to know them."

As the car pulled into a long circular drive leading to the porte-cochere of a high old one-story house, John began to wonder again if all this were real, or a crazy dream. The blue hortensias, the feathery pink acacias. Would he wake and find himself back in New York?

"Looks cockeyed to me," he muttered, and when Sarah turned with a questioning smile, he went on: "That house leans slightly toward the east. See?"

"Said to be haunted," said Mrs. Shaw, happily.

"Don't doubt it," muttered John.

Now their attention was taken by the noble figure, patient and erect in a black calico dress, which waited on the front veranda. It was a very old black woman with a few grizzled white curls escaping from under her cap.

"Mawnin', Tanager," said Mrs. Shaw, suddenly lapsing into a theatrical lawsy-me-shut-my-mouf accent. "Heah is Miz Morgana's frens from the Nawth."

"Welcome," said Tanager, serenely as a sibyl, inclining her head formally and speaking perfectly good English. "I have biscuits waiting."

"I'll leave you here," said Mrs. Shaw in a hushed voice, but resuming her natural tone as Tanager went inside. "Tanager and I just don't operate on the same wavelength, you know, but listen, I'm always at the station, come have morning cokes with me. And—good luck!" They all shook hands and she went back to her car.

After lunch of baked ham, cucumber salad, and hot biscuits, even John relented a little, and began to study the paintings crowding each other on the dark walls of the dining room.

"Thas Miz Morgana with her pony at seven years old," Tanager informed them, and "thas Miz Morgana when she was a Maid in the Mobile Mardi Gras, and this is her signing the contract with her publisher. Thas for her first book, she has written 'bout a dozen. Now, take these window shades—" Here Tanager smiled impishly, pointing with her thin black finger to one of the blue canvas shades at the dining room windows. "Miz Morgana always tells the spring tourists that these here were made from the uniforms of Yankee soldier boys killed in the garden by her grandmother, but truth is, they came out the Montgomery Ward catalogue for 19 and 23. I know, I went to the station help collect them. We saved the cardboard rolls they came in and painted them red to be candles for the Christmas decorations on the lawn. I always tell her, Miz Morgana, I say, when you are not making stories, you just plain making fibs. Ha, ha, and she is, too."

"I don't doubt it," said John, thinking to himself how much he loathed Morgana, sight unseen.

"A nap wouldn't hurt," said Sarah, guessing his reaction.

After the initial exploration, requiring several days, of house and grounds, which were discovered to be spacious, untidy, and very pleasant, John settled himself at the library desk, after removing china cats, vases, a bronze lamp shaped like a monkey, a signed photograph of Frances Parkinson Keyes, and a *Nouveau Petit Larousse Illustré*. He had letters and reviews to write.

Sarah, meantime, let loose after more than twenty years in a Manhattan apartment, save for conventional summer junketings, could scarcely be persuaded to come indoors. The turbulent richness of the Alabama autumn, all lushly green but touched by the exuberance of goldenrod and asters assembled along the roads, had captivated her.

"John!" she cried, bursting through the French windows into the library. "Come look at these callicarpas! Just come look!"

But he only said peevishly: "Do you indeed 'come from haunts of coot and . . . callicarpa?"

Sarah only smiled. She was happy, already had a tan.

So days went quietly, about five of them, until, with that particular ironical sense Fate so often conjures when she underlines a supposition, a fancy, a whim, a hint, and makes them into a fact, something happened that made John and Sarah begin to believe that *Glynrose* could indeed be haunted.

One night they were wakened from a deep peaceful country

sleep by a series of creaks and a kind of ticking sound. They woke simultaneously and listened with beating hearts. The sound came from the library, repeated at irregular intervals.

"Sounds like a time bomb," whispered Sarah, always romantic.

"Have you ever heard one?" enquired John. "Besides, Morgana can't hate me that much for her only bad review."

But the sound continued faintly but clearly in the chill of the night. Sarah shivered and reached for her wrapper. "I knew we should never have come here," said John, loathing the idea of getting up, yet knowing well that the myth of male gallantry and courage required that he flick on the lights and report nothing to be seen in the library. Grumbling he rose, followed by Sarah, who would not be left alone. They stumbled across the hall, turned on all the lights in the library, and listened . . . to nothing. The sounds had stopped.

"Oh, well," he muttered, "back to bed." So they did. But once comfortably settled the sounds began again, faintly at first, then more loudly and at longer intervals. But John and Sarah listened in silence, wondering how much was fear rub-a-dub-dubbing past their eardrums, and thinking one might become accustomed and go back to sleep.

"Old houses always creak," observed Sarah, drowsily. "Unless it's a deathwatch beetle."

"But that sounds like somebody working on something," said John. They listened long, but the sounds were gone.

"Don't say anything about it to Tanager," cautioned Sarah as they took places at the breakfast table. "She may really believe in ghosts."

"I shouldn't be surprised if she didn't make those sounds herself," sniffed John. "I bet old H.H. hires her to keep us awake. He was pretty p.o.'d at my review of Morgana's book, after all. I mean, sending us South and all, as a result. God help us, Sarah, if we survive all this, we'll never go south of Manhattan Island again as long as we live."

"But I like our restaurant in Philadelphia," she said wistfully.

Two nights later the sounds were heard again, were even more unnerving. A slow splintering or shattering was suggested, and John and Sarah, now really troubled, stared at one another by moonlight sifting through the pecan tree into their room. Again they rose cautiously, again the sounds stopped when they entered the library, again the morning found them puffy-eyed for loss of sleep.

"Let's go see Mrs. Shaw,"suggested Sarah. "She's the only logical person around."

"Wondered when I'd see you," smiled Mrs. Shaw. "That Tanager is a great cook, I thought maybe she had you tablebound." She opened Coca-Colas expertly, with loud *blops!* and served them.

"I have something to show you," she said, pulling a roll of paper from under the counter, "that'll interest you." She unrolled a large mezzotint of an antebellum mansion amidst formal gardens, fashionable couples strolling through the trees.

"It's *Glynrose* in 1830," she explained enthusiastically. "See, this is the old house that was destroyed in The War. The house that Morgana's father moved here, one you're in now, stands here." She indicated the formal gardens dominated by a huge old cowcumber magnolia tree with a bench around the trunk.

"Where did you find it?" asked John.

"Bought it off a tenant farmer when I was giving my questionnaire. Charming, isn't it?"

"Are you going to sell it to Morgana?" asked Sarah, studying the quaint figures in the print, thinking she'd like it herself.

"Lord, no!" exclaimed Mrs. Shaw. "I'll keep it for a souvenir of Palmyra Junction. I've gotten quite fascinated with the local history. I've dug up lots of stuff; I might even try my hand at an historical novel after I finish my doctorate."

John groaned, then recollecting what had brought them to the station, told Mrs. Shaw about their ghostly noises.

"You're absolutely certain," she said, rearranging her blue bandanna, "that it's not just atmospheric conditions? Old timbers, you know."

"Those sounds . . . they seem, you know, as if they were directed by something intelligent . . . sounds like somebody working . . ."

"What does Tanager say?" asked Mrs. Shaw.

"We were afraid to ask her . . . didn't want to frighten her."

"Nonsense," said Mrs. Shaw firmly. "Tanager is very religious. She could confront all the devils in Hell more adequately than any of us. Ask her what to do."

So they sought out Tanager and told her about the sounds.

"It's a mixed ghost," she said at once.

"What's that?"

"See . . . that's when a soul is peaceful, but has cast off a burden of pure-dee meanness before leaving this earth. Time six or eight folks have left their meannesses roaming around at night, all those meannessess get together and make a mixed ghost. That kind of ghost never has a name, and never harms children."

"What could it do to us?" asked Sarah.

"Oh, I'm not worried about you, Mrs. Hobbins, but . . ." her eyes lit up mischievously, "I'd like to think how to guard Mr. Hobbins, for he does have a heap of mortal pride."

"I bet," blurted John, but not unhumorously, "you make those noises."

"I promise you on my name of Tanager," said the old woman imperiously, "that if I chose to go 'round rousing up the night, I'd have such a fright of clanking chains it'd take a wheelbarrow to tote them back and forth. No, I sleep.

I've raised my children, sent them all to school, made my peace with the good Lord, and make a very light pastry: I sleep of a night."

That night the sounds were heard again, despite the Cross of Salt which Tanager carefully arranged on the polished parquetry of the library floor. This time it seemed an almost inaudible groan or whine could be heard under the ghostly tapping. John jumped out of bed, furious, and stormed into the library.

"Show yourself, you damn old mixed ghost!" he shouted.

"Sssh!" said Sarah. "I might as well make coffee, since we're not going to sleep."

They spent the night drinking coffee and looking at Morgana's old photograph albums. John decided they should leave the next day, but Sarah said he simply couldn't let down the Women's Club, which had shanghaied him as the "entertainment" for their regular monthly evening function. Resigned, John agreed.

Mr. and Mrs. Castex were the hosts for the Women's Club meeting. The host was frankly and jovially drunk when John and Sarah arrived. The door was opened for them by the pretty blonde seen at the station, then in shorts and lanky-haired, now upswept and in drifts of blue tulle.

"Hey," she said, and opened wide the door.

"Hello, Mr. Huggins, Mrs. Huggins," mouthed Mr. Castex.

"Hobbins," corrected the pretty blonde. "Daddy, you're crocked."

Heads turned, other doors opened, bevies of ladies came to greet the celebrity and to compliment his wife: "You must have a *fascinating* life being married to such a famous man! Does he really read *all* those books; I bet you have a hard time getting him to the table! I don't always read all the books, but I *do* read a lot of Mr. Hobbins' reviews!" As

Sarah fought her way in she saw a coterie of husbands clustered around the sideboard where the liquor bottles gleamed.

"I hope you have a simply ravenous appetite, Mr. Hobbins," beamed a portly gray-haired lady over her corsage bouquet of seven yellow orchids, "because Bessabee has made those croquettes you may have heard about, even 'way up theah in the Nawth."

"This'll help, Mr. Hudgins," said Mr. Castex, proffering a tall glass.

"Hobbins," said the blonde girl.

"I'll say," murmured John, burying his nose in the drink.

"Shame Morgana can't be here," a pale lady cried out several times to different people.

"Mary Fosdick, come quick! Help me see to these muffins!" came a voice from the kitchen, and the portly lady moved with grandeur toward the back of the house, her movements accompanied by a backwash sibilancy from hidden taffetas.

"Is the name Hudgins or Huggins?" a lanky old gentleman was asking Sarah when the front door burst open and there stood a wild-eyed lady in a white satin hoopskirt and a red wool jacket. Her arms were laden with a huge bouquet of goldenrod and Turk's Cap lilies.

"Listen," she put the question to the assemblage, notably to John who was nearest, "is tonight the man talking on flower arrangement or is tonight the man about books?"

"Books, I'm afraid," replied John, feeling good for no reason, and essaying a rueful smile he had not used since years before when in the folly of youth he had first seen and attempted to imitate Leslie Howard.

"Oh!" cried the wild-eyed lady, "then Greggie was right!"

She stood aside for her husband to enter, a stocky man with a florid complexion. "You were right, Greggie, I swear. I was so sure." Then she turned to John and gave him a wide grin. "I always like to bring something *appropriate* to give to the speaker and I was sure tonight was Flower Arrangement. I don't know what I could bring *you*, anyway. I never wrote a book."

"Well, did you ever read one?" asked John very charmingly, and the wild-eyed lady roared with glee. Sarah clutched her glass and thought, they may all be innocents here, but one can go too far, even so. But now the lady's husband stepped forward, checking a wicked chuckle deep in his throat, to take John's hand and shake it.

"Monnie reads *True Passion* and *Home Carpenter*, and that's about it," he laughed.

"That don' keep me from bringing something appropriate to give the speaker," said the lady, still shaken with laughter. "Everybody *knows* I always bring something appropriate."

John, appalled at the possibilities, was just backing away and musing, "What if I were taking part in a debate on abortion?" when the lady turned and dumped her armload of flowers into his protesting hands.

"There, there, old smarty, take 'em anyway, and press 'em in your books," she giggled, then made her way toward the sideboard. "Who's bartender?" she shouted.

"All right now!" sang out Mrs. Castex, arriving from the sun parlor where the tables were laid. "Let's get this show on the road. We're going to have *Moonlight Sonata*, second movement, from Anne Rubicam, then Jerry Bobo will favor us with a tap dance. Then we'll have our piece duh ruhsistance . . . " and here she smiled at John cowering in his chair surrounded by flowers and mutely begging moral support from Sarah.

Afterwards, well-liquored and well-fed, as he locked the door of *Glynrose* against the world, John suddenly laughed out loud, causing Sarah to stop dead still and fix him with a look.

"That was fun," he said.

"Well, yes, it was," said Sarah, amazed.

"Let's have a nightcap," he suggested, tugging at his shoes.

"Okay," she agreed.

So they put the tray on the bedside table and had a choice two-hour postmortem of the party, vying to recollect the choicer bits of conversation. Finally, pleasantly exhausted, they fell asleep, and that's when the ghost made its biggest and best appearance.

John and Sarah woke to a tremendous and shattering explosion which reverberated over the silent night-heavy hills, shook the house, and was followed by a whole orchestra of lesser sounds: broken glass falling, birds awakened and chattering sleepily in the trees outside, finally the diminishing tinkle of crystal chandeliers jangling then slowly growing still.

"My God, what is it?" cried Sarah.

"Come on!" cried John, leaping from bed, and running into the hall. The library door was open and cautiously he put his hand inside and flicked the light switch. The two chandeliers blazed with light, the pendants still swaying slightly, and they saw a crazy sight and stood there silent, wonderingly.

The room was in total disorder around a hole in the floor about eight feet across. Morgana's desk had half slid into the gap, arrested by a beam. Bits of parquetry were everywhere, and two windowpanes broken. But out of the black hole, a strange object reared up into the room. A tree of coiled black branches bearing a few leathery old leaves and and a few pale ghostly new ones. They tiptoed toward the hole and looked in. They saw a great black stump, cut almost at ground level, from one side of which rose a lesser stump which in its time—who knows how many years or decades before?—had also been cut. From the opposite side rose the new growth, the tortuously curved trunk and boughs which had pushed against the floor until it yielded. The stump was sooty black and the black earth about it was touched with a green-gold mold. The branches were dingy black too, save for the pale leaf-stems and buds on the tips. They smelt a rich odor of damp earth.

They heard footsteps and Tanager appeared wrapped in a multicolored afghan which covered her head and shoulders and hung to her knees. She had come from her cottage on the corner of the estate, dazed with sleep. She wandered to the brink of the hole and looked down.

"Magnolia tree," she crooned, nodding. "Magnolia tree." Then she looked about her at the disordered room. "Tomorrow," she mumbled and went back out again.

John, recovering his voice, kicked at the branches which had raised themselves about four feet into the room. "This tears it," he shouted. "This is the end, this does it!" But Sarah had picked up a loose bit of parquetry, already had chosen her souvenir of Palmyra Junction.

"Let's pack!" cried John. "We've had it!"

The morning light found them fishing in the hole in the floor with a contraption they'd made of bent coat hangers. They succeeded at last in fishing up John's notebooks which had fallen down there. Only when their packed luggage reposed in the front hall did they learn from Tanager that there were no trains until the next day.

But Mrs. Shaw, learning by grapevine of the prodigy, came running, smartly attired in a tweed suit and forgetting her disguise.

"What a story!" she said. "You can sell this to the *News Mirror.* Cut down twice and still full of life. Cut and come again!"

"All I want," said John quietly, "is to get the hell out of here. Visitors are coming up the walk this very instant to see our freak."

They were too: the Castexes with their daughter, once

more in shorts, and the wild-eyed lady of the appropriate. John craned nervously to see what she might be carrying.

"Listen," said Mrs. Shaw. "I'll borrow a bandanna from Tanager and drive you up to Demopolis to catch the 12:15. I was so excited I forgot my Mandy costume."

"If you so dead-set to leave," said Tanager, coming in with a basket, "you better go the side way, leave me at the front door to charge admission. But just you take this lap-lunch."

They took it and fled. But Fate was at the station in Demopolis. She came in on the 12:15 from Mobile.

"Age of Marvels!" exclaimed Mrs. Shaw, as, after exchanging addresses, they moved toward the train just pulling in. A vision in purple and veils was unfolding itself from the Pullman wagon: Morgana it was, home from the West with somewhat brighter red hair, somewhat darker lashes, and seven yards of violet tulle floating about her head and shoulders.

"Goodbye and good luck," laughed Mrs. Shaw. "I'm leaving, I don't want any part of that girl. Gotta run get into my working togs. See you someday in New York. *Ciao!*"

But Morgana, quick as a shot, saw the retreating Mrs. Shaw, sized up John and Sarah, and knew instantly who they were. She fairly lept from the train.

"John Hobbins, you naughty man!" she intoned in a rich mezzo-soprano, a road-company Carmen. "How could you ever write such mean things about me? Why, we've never even met till this red hot minute! Though Cousin H.H. says you are really a very naughty man, that's what he says."

"Mrs. Hadley, my wife Sarah."

"Hello, hon. I hope you enjoyed drafty old *Glynrose!*"

"Unforgettable experience," said Sarah suavely, but added, "I think we should tell you . . . "

"Tell me nothing! No time! Here you are getting on and me getting off . . . ships that pass in the night! Oh, well, I'll see you in New York in April. But this time I'm not going to give you a chance, no indeed. This time you'll read my novel *before* it's published and tell me what you think is wrong, not write about me in the *News-Forum* in that nasty way *afterwards*. Here, boy!" She seized a valise from the porter, rested it on a tomato crate, unlocked and rummaged.

"Awwwahboooaaad!" said the stationmaster.

"Here!" cried Morgana triumphantly, and pushed six hundred neatly typed pages at John who took them as if drugged while Sarah pushed him into the train. Glancing down he saw the title: *Around the World on Tiptoe, a Novel of the Ballet.* Visibly paler, he turned to the window. Morgana was waving all seven yards of tulle cheerily.

"Write and tell me what you think!" she shouted. "You know the address of my old ruin!"

John laughed hysterically as the train pulled out. And all the way North he twitched, stared moodily at the landscape, wouldn't eat Tanager's picnic lunch, made Sarah worry.

"Down to the puritan marrow of my bones . . ." he quoted.

In New York they all thought John looked splendid after his much envied rest in the South, but then one day when the *Advance News of New Books* carried across its cover the legend "New Wine from an Old Vineyard" and inside revealed a double-page spread from a major publisher ballyhooing three new novels by three new Southern authors, all under 21, with their pictures . . . John went early to lunch and never returned to the office. It made quite a stir at the time, but people had almost forgotten about him when it came out that he had gone to Connecticut and started a new life with an insurance company.

Mrs. Dorothy Shaw, after the treatise which won her her doctorate, wrote an historical novel, *Tree of Fury*, under the pen name Palmyra Glyn. This became a highly successful film, and at last word, was being turned into a musical show called *Stars in the Branches* by a well-known composer librettist team.

And Sarah, patient Sarah, finally had a house up in Connecticut and there in her garden coaxed two small magnolia trees to achieve a Southern flourish and grandeur, but naturally they wouldn't. Wrong climate.

Biscuits

Mobile, April, 1873

Eveline had her feet up on the chaise longue. She hummed an Offenbach waltz to herself; she'd heard it the night before at a thrillingly late musicale and collation. The old port of Mobile always received the latest sheet music and fashion reviews from Paris, the latest books from London. Eveline sighed with pleasure. She looked at her hands: so clean, the nails so well tended. She remembered vividly how they'd looked only a year ago, up-country, when she and her mother had tried to keep up the kitchen garden at Weymouth Plantation. And just when the sweet corn was bearing, and pecks of okra, eggplant, squash, and beans had been picked, why, if the Yankee supply officers hadn't come over from the barracks, confiscating it all. Paying good money, of course, but nothing to eat anywhere for Eveline and her mother to buy, save weevily meal and clammy flour. But they'd borne it, and survived on plantation bread, skillet bread, journey cake, wild blackberries, and some sweet pepers which by chance grew behind the empty chicken sheds.

Eveline looked up and sniffed the air. Out in the kitchen Moddy was cooking a succulent ratty-too of the first vegetables, the *primeurs.* Or "preemers," as she said.

"Much better the second day, iffen I can keep your greedy

paws outen it," Moddy had told her as she chopped onions.

Eveline had never really had enough to eat throughout her childhood and youth. And it wasn't only the war. She was the last of seven children; her father had died when she was two. By the time the Sunday platter reached her, she was lucky to have a fragment of chicken wing, once in a while the neck. Eveline's widowed mother had depended on the boys to help her, but when the War started, they'd gone off one by one. Her brother Tarry, one year older than Eveline, had been prodigious in catching fish and hunting squirrel and wild turkey, but when two of his older brothers had died in battle he'd gone off too, to fight the "Yankee varmints." Her sisters had married and Eveline was left with her mother in the silent hulk of a house, dreaming, whether awake or asleep, of the dishes described in her Grandmother Rapier's fine-penned household books.

Eveline sniffed the air again: onion, garlic, peppers, eggplant, celery, tomatoes. She looked about the room vaguely. She knew she should be sewing, or unpacking the last trunks, putting her new household in order.

But she was plum worn out. Since morning, the neighbor ladies and the church ladies had come to call, bringing napkin-covered trays and platters, formally welcoming the new young minister's new wife. Since morning, Eveline had received them with her gentle smile and soft-spoken repeated, "How thoughtful of you," and "You are truly kind," and "Ah, but I am so grateful." Now she was weary.

"I could," she thought, with a sudden achingly sweet sense of power, "call out to Moddy and she'd bring me a glass of port and a benne-seed wafer." She concentrated on the marvel of this fact, and decided to contemplate it before putting her power into effect.

How suddenly things had put themselves right in a world which had seemed all chaos and grayness to her. She remembered how her mother had begun to go quirky and remembered things from her childhood but not where she'd hid the key to the physick box. How the river had flooded last spring and ruined their first plantings. How in the storm an oak had crashed and ruined the kitchen wing. Not enough food, no clothes, no music, no books, no prospects, the occupying Yankee soldiers smirking at her when she had to walk the two miles into town to post letters or buy seed. Then Garrett, her distant cousin from Savannah, had turned up, newly ordained, witty and High Church, posted to Mobile, on his way with the Bishop's words ringing in his ears.

"My dear boy, you must find a nice little wife for yourself. Mobile is a dangerous place for a well-favored saucy youth like you . . . and you know all those wicked French from Demopolis have gone down there to teach the violin, and dancing, and have opened card parlors and established more private . . . more arduous . . . centers of diversion . . . you'd best find a wife. . . "

And Garrett had quite simply fallen in love with his slim, quiet, velvet-eyed cousin Eveline. "Psyche . . . " he thought, enchanted, "but her eyes are Hera's. . . "

Eveline had floated through it all in a daze, not believing it was happening to her. Her mother had concentrated long enough to go and pry a punch bowl and some heavy old spoons from a hollow in the wall under the stairs to the kitchen loft, but couldn't remember where they'd hid the knives and forks.

"It'll come back to me," she said hopefully. "Now Eveline, don't forget to take a good bug powder when you go to Mobile. You don't know whether your bed will be infested or not. In your new house be sure to get the best new mattress, and even so purify it with rose water and peppercorns . . . a good night's sleep is worth a few sneezes, I always say . . . and if your mattress is stuffed with Spanish Moss, likely as not it'll be swarming with chiggers . . . God protect us!"

Eveline smiled at the recollection of her mother, then sighed and looked at her clean ladylike hands. Why, I'll never have to turn back a coverlet, much less purify a mattress. As for digging in the dirt, banish the thought forever . . . unless, she corrected herself, I take a notion to set out some cuttings of Grand Duke jessamine. She wriggled her toes in her shoes, then glanced over her shoulder. The parlor tables were covered with the napkin-covered plates the ladies had brought. She looked toward the dining table in the next room: more white shapes. She could see, outside in the back yard, Elwyn prodding the cauldron of wash with a wooden stave. She watched Elwyn add wood to the fire and shave some lye soap into the cauldron, then Eveline's gaze returned to the dining-room table. Her first thought was that she should clear it. It was already eleven o'clock; Garrett would be home to eat at noon. But Moddy will clear the table, she thought.

Suddenly she rose and went to a round damask-covered parlor table. She lifted a napkin on a tray: buttermilk biscuits, still slightly warm. She tried other platters, went on to the dining-room sideboard, the table. Beaten biscuits, Stratford biscuits, corn muffins, Avendaw muffins, Cherokee biscuits, Creole calettes, galettas, soda biscuits, journey cake, finger bread, white pones, yellow pones . . . by now Eveline was frowning.

She stared into the back yard. Elwyn had vanished from sight, the steam rose from the wash pot.

"Miz Eveline?"

She had not heard Moddy come padding in, in her straw scuffs, her stern face framed by a white turban.

"What is it, Moddy?"

"Mister Larken passed by, says he's butchering tomorrow,

gonna bring you a fine roast, some steaks, and a nice passel of ribs."

"That'll be nice," said Eveline vaguely, but an image took shape in her mind, part Christmas, part Mardi Gras. She could almost smell the roast, and her ribs and breasts seemed suddenly constrained, too tightly laced into her stays.

She sighed, caught her breath.

"Mr. Finch's boy brought the beer and the ratafia; says the boat's in and they'll be unloading the Madeira in the mawnin'. Ten cases is picked out for yawl."

"Mr. Garrett will be pleased," murmured Eveline.

"Sho' will," laughed Moddy. "Them young fellows of the cloth can really put it away, now cain't they. Ho!"

Moddy had already gone before Eveline looked up again from contemplating the dishes and salvers covering every surface. For one instant she thought of the smoke-blackened kitchens at Weymouth Plantation and of the minute shrivelled corpses of weevils in the cornbread. She giggled nervously, and pushed back an erring curl.

Suddenly she came to life.

A few bird-like flicks of her head as once more she glanced at all those napkin-covered dishes. Then she glided out into the hall and reached for her handsome Paisley hanging on the rack, thought better of it and took down an old black knotted shawl which had been her Granny's. She put it around her, picked up her flower basket, and returned to the living room. Deftly, swiftly, she dumped the biscuits and pones into her basket. When it was full, she let herself out the front door and went down the iron steps into the garden.

Very carefully she began to impale a biscuit or pone on each iron spear of the fence which surrounded the house, both on the St. Anthony Street side, and on the North Jackson Street side.

When her basket was empty she ran back inside and filled

it again. Then back outside again, sticking a piece of bread on each spike. She turned to look back along the fence, studying the effect, laughed gaily. When she'd garnished every protuberance on the fence, she tossed what bread was left under the elephant ears and skipped up the stairs, singing under her breath a bawdy soldiers' song she'd learned by eavesdropping on her brothers. She didn't bother to look back when she heard gasps from the first passerby. She went on inside and looked at herself in the mirror for a long while.

Africa

Every man has his own Africa.
Dr. S. Willoughby

Mr. Dan was black, not brown-black, nor blue-black. He was like the pigment in the paint boxes called "ivory black." Black ivory. He was tall, extremely slim, but well formed, not skinny. He moved with such casual grace that his footfall made no sound. He seemed severe until he smiled, then all Africa smiled.

He had always been called "Mr. Dan" because of his courtly ways and high courtesy. He was servant to the Mannheim and Faber clans, in their big old house on Government Street in Mobile. They adored him. When untidy cigar smokers were absently flicking ashes into space, his long alpaca-clad arm would suddenly appear as if materializing from another dimension, holding an ashtray under the offending cigar. Mr. Dan did not smoke, hated the smell of cigars.

"Hell's not sulphur," he claimed. "Sulphur is gonna purify. Oh, no. Hell is all the lawyers and bank directors and tugboat captains sitting in a closed room under the ground, smoking cigars."

When Mr. Dan found any foodstuffs or dry goods wanting in quality, he'd assume a lofty expression and intone, "Looks like it was sent for and couldn't come."

He was a repository of home remedies. For colds he'd recommend, "More bourbon than honey, and more honey than lemon," a delicious medicine. When the children were fretting to leave the table before the end of a meal, or wanting to rush outside without finishing the minor household tasks required of them, he'd admonish, "Unh-unh, no you don't. Church ain't out till the fat lady sings."

He kept the other servants in line, especially a high-yaller piece of impudence called Florrie. She was in love with him, but he never gave her a tumble. The milk-chocolate cook, Ottilie, adored Mr. Dan and always "kept back" some splendid morsel for him.

Mr. Dan had gone off as a soldier in the First World War, and afterwards had tales of France and Alsace to tell. They were picturesque accounts of young soldiers' pranks, of the big drunken fete the night of the Armistice, of storms on the Atlantic. But one story puzzled folks in Mobile and, finally, by its improbability, caused Mr. Dan to lose much of his prestige.

He claimed he had been in Africa . . . or rather, that he had seen it.

"See, I climbed up this hill . . . wasn't too high . . . had all kinda trees like you never seen . . . and I looked out over all that low ground like you never seen . . . and I looked out over that low ground down over there and I could see Africa . . . I saw the elephants . . . and the gee-raffs . . . and them mean little ole hyenas, and a hunnert . . . no, two hunnert . . . different kinds of animals . . . all strutting around, knowing they owned the place . . . 'cause they did . . . Africa. . . "

"Why, Mr. Dan," they'd say. "You know you didn't go to Africa. You served in France, and well, Alsace, but you didn't go to Africa."

Tiny old Miss Faber, perceptive and clever, would try to reason out Mr. Dan's tale.

"But, suppose . . . " she'd muse, "he had a weekend leave or a few days' leave and ended up on Gibraltar where they have those monkeys . . . and Africa *is* just across the Straits of Gibraltar . . . and you *can* see it from up on the Rock." She questioned him.

"Mr. Dan," she asked. "Did you take a boat? How long did it take you to get to Africa?"

By then, years after the war, he was extremely cautious in speaking of this experience.

"Like I done tol' you, Miss Laura. I walked a long way, walked and walked along the river . . . then I saw these tall trees with white flowers and I went over there and walked some more and came to these hills . . . and I saw Africa . . . rivers too. . . "

"Well," said Dr. Maury at dinner one night, when they'd been going over it for the umpteenth time. "It might be a vision, a longed-for image of what for him was his own, his promised land. With the primitive mentality, it's easy to confuse the imagined and the factual."

But who could think of Mr. Dan as "primitive"? I couldn't. He was a gentleman of color, and more mentally alert than many gentlemen of whatsoever color.

In the 1920s the Confederate earthworks, thrown up for the defense of Mobile during the War Between the States, still stood at the end of Lafayette Street. A Bosch landscape of red clay hummocks, trenches, pines, and tangles of smilax and the newly imported kudzu. Children loved to play there, to dig ovens in the hard clay embankments and roast potatoes and sausages. An old conjure man named Belbar lived deeper into the woods with his goat Clara and his numberless cats. Black people went to consult him and to buy the gris-gris he made, charms effective in matters of love or money, for protection against enemies, to lure the indifferent, all that. White children seldom penetrated the woods as far as Belbar's corrugated tin shack, but we often saw black servants we knew strolling through the gullies and hummocks to Belbar.

Once, straying deep into the woods, seeking ladies' watches and polygalas, I heard a rhythmic chant off through the trees, that plaintive jubilancy of black song when they're singing for themselves. Cautiously I placed my basket under a tree and I climbed a steep bank, approaching the summit under cover of a thick stand of willow oak, redolent in the hot stillness. In a clearing a group of maybe ten blacks were sitting around with their picnic baskets; one or two of the older women had white sun umbrellas. Umbrellas, not parasols. As Mr. Dan once explained, "Don't you see . . . they's a difference . . . umbrellas bend down and make a shade, parasols is flat, they just keep the sun off."

They were all singing, with one wiry little old woman chiming in with an acid high soprano which gives that "other" feeling, a music every Southerner knows. And Mr. Dan was dancing. He danced on his right leg. His left foot was pressed against the side of his right knee; he never put his left foot down. His arms made sinuous curving motions, balancing him as he turned and hopped, but giving no sign of being what balanced him. Their song was something like this:

"Ka-bel-ba . . . ah!
Ka-bel-ba . . . ah!
Ka-mamba-bel-ba . . . ah, ah, ah!
Namba-bel-ba . . . ah!
Kanamba-bel-ba . . . ah!
Ka-bel-kamamba . . . ah, ah, ah!"

Mr. Dan, tall, concentrated, a tiny smile curling his lips, danced weightlessly around the clearing on one foot.

But the acid soprano saw me and said to the others, "Uh-oh,

here comes anudden just like th' udden. . . " the standard warning among blacks when whites are approaching. They all stopped singing and remained motionless, while Mr. Dan finished a circle then stood still.

"How did you know we was here?" Mr. Dan asked mildly.

"I . . . I heard you singing . . . I didn't mean to butt in . . . I'm going back now," I stammered, feeling I had seen something I shouldn't.

Whereupon Mean-Mouth Mama, who worked for the Turners, said nastily, "Heard us? Why, chile, you live at 50 South Bayou Street. A fur piece! Ain't he sensible? So sensible he kin hear us all dem blocks away? *Sensible!* Why, he could hear him a mouse fartin' in a trunk in a closet in a closed house across the Bay!"

Everybody laughed and I nodded apologetically and climbed back down the slope. I sat down with my basket under a tallowberry tree and I thought, "Mr. Dan must really have been in Africa. That was an African dance, it's bound to be." I remembered a photograph in our geography book in Miss Enderle's class, a picture of a tall, lean man like Mr. Dan, with one leg propped up against the other like that, reminding one of cranes and ibises.

"Mr. Dan must have gone to Africa!"

But his story was never believed, and it became a standard joke. "Tell us about when you went to Africa. . . " they'd say to him, with a knowing smile. Mr. Dan never lost his dignity nor his good humor. He told his tale, always the same way. But he had lost face somehow and some of the little girls went so far as to skip rope to an old rhyme from way back when, to tease him:

"Ole Uncle Dan was a fine ole man,
Washed his face in a frying pan,
Combed his hair with a wagon wheel,
Died with a toothache in his heel."

I could only shake my head and think, "But he *did* go to Africa."

And so did I. At least, I went to Mr. Dan's Africa. Centuries later, when I went to school in Paris after the Second World War, I lunched Chez Marius in Rue Fossé St. Bernard, and afterwards, effulgently digestive, went strolling. I went past the now-vanished *Halles des vins* and went on until I came to a big gate. It was a park, full of flowering shrubs, strollers, lovers, children with nurses. I strolled on to where a path rose toward a little hill; I followed it to higher ground. I found rare trees with metal plaques informing who had planted them and when. I found beds of forget-me-nots by a little pond with two gliding swans. I sat on a bench and looked out and there . . . below me . . . was Africa. Mr. Dan's Africa, I mean. And mine. I was in the *Jardin des Plantes,* the Paris botanical gardens with its menagerie which began with the animals from the royal collection at Versailles, brought here after the Revolution.

I could see a young elephant stretching his trunk over his enclosure fence to pick a *magnolia grandiflora,* I could see two giraffes rubbing their necks together, clouds of monkeys being gregarious, picking salt flakes from each other's scalps. Some distant brown forms, unidentifiable, a bear, some squawking bright-colored birds. I reached down idly and picked up some chips of rose-colored granite from a flower bed; I put them in my pocket.

Seven years later, back in Mobile, I sought out Mr. Dan's grave in the black cemetery. After a while I found it, a flat stone with the name DANILO FORBES and dates. I took those chips of rose stone from my pocket and laid them there, carefully.

"Ça va, Daniel?" I asked, softly.

Palladian Style

Fontanelle was the name of the house. It was built about 1801, over in Sophia County, near the border of Baldwin County. There was a lovely spring in the garden. It fed a deep ferny stream bed, no more than a ditch, which meandered on under the oaks and green bays to join Binn's Creek about half a mile away. The house had seen bad days. After the defeat of the South, the family which owned *Fontanelle* had moved to Paris (where they had money) and never returned. It passed to cousins who were too poor to repair the place and live in it. It had sheltered hunters, then a family of squatters, then fell empty, derelict, stinking of rot and human feces, at last home for bats and beetles. Then, in the way that a hurricane-felled tree will suddenly send up a strong straight new growth from the roots, a young man of the inheriting family, a student of architecture, decided to restore the place. Factories had been built a few miles away, new roads passed not too far off, and the South had begun to take self-conscious delight in receiving tourists from the outer world: that region, as they figured it, of haste, waste, and bickering outside the Flowery Kingdom.

Eric, the architect, personally waded the spring and stream bed to dig out old shoes, beer cans, the most unwonted objects. He got a bank loan, worked for a year, and one day there was the handsome *Fontanelle* reborn, paint-sassy, inviting.

Fontanelle said the sign, real gold-leaf italics on a sturdy white enamel board. Eric was at the gatehouse, to deal with parking and selling tickets. He had prevailed on three childhood friends who happened to be on hand to dress in antebellum costume, as is often the custom in the South when houses are opened to visitors. So the girls were "receiving" in hoopskirts and Winterhalter hats.

Maude Anne Aikens, recently engaged, was the mildest of the three; her job was to punch the admittance tickets. She had a charming pointed face, a solemn air, but had written some excellent limericks of wildest obscenity, circulated only in her immediate circle, which included her two old school friends who sat with her now on the high, wide veranda. She herself was standing, carefully painting her long nails a candy pink.

Miroslava Dobbs was the beauty of the group. She had flawless skin, blue-grey eyes which changed color every hour on the hour, and honey-blonde hair which took its gleam from the old-fashioned "one hundred strokes a day." She was the total personification of what is usually meant by "Southern girl." Mind you, no two people will agree on what that means (Scarlett! Blanche! Regina!) but, anyway, she had a purring voice, clean fingernails, tiny waist, a titanic appetite for life on all levels, perfect charm of manner. Yes, a sex-pot. But what she thought was her own business. Wounding glances and a positively assassinating smile. She had come home for a visit after medical studies in New York. She was swinging lazily on the porch, holding a highball in lace-mitted hands, bourbon bottle and water pitcher discreetly hidden amidst the ferns. She was the upstairs guide.

The third young woman, the downstairs guide, Pee-Wee Sutcliffe, sat in a rocker, energetically rocking, swinging her feet up happily. She had eaten a pecan and the bits of shell, under her rockers, crunchy-crunch, seemed to say "Billy-boy, Billy-boy, Billy-boy!" which was what she was thinking, having designs on Billy Mayhall. She was home from Paris, after three years in school, and would go back for a last year of study. Paris had given her that tenderly knowing look some Russian refugees have: how can you possibly understand if you didn't live in old St. Petersburg? Thus, for her, Paris. She was telling the others about an adventure with a priest in mufti on the train for Marseilles.

"Did you know he was a priest?"

"How could I?" protested Pee-Wee. "He was wearing a tweed suit!"

"And you were alone with him in the compartment?"

"Yes . . . that was the real reason it was exciting. He'd been giving me the glad eye the whole trip, while I looked out the window or pretended to read *The Naked Ape*. There was an awful old sour puss lady in there with us, and she got off about thirty minutes before Marseilles. I knew it was then or never. He'd got me boiling the way he never took those eyes off me. They were like black olives."

"What'd you do?"

"Put the book away and stretched, stretched, stretched. Then took my shoes off . . . so he leapt at me . . . it was wonderful."

"You mean he . . . did frilly-quiffs?"

"No, no!"

"Oh," said Maude Anne, her polish brush poised, "you must mean twiddly-fingers."

"Unh-unh!"

"Then . . ." mused Miroslava, "was it . . . missionary position?"

"No!" laughed Pee-Wee.

"Ah!" went on Miroslava. "Then it was *lingua franca!*"

"Yes," sighed Pee-Wee. "It was . . . heavenly."

"Yawl are awful," drawled Maude Anne. "Bawds! Just a bunch of bawds! I'm so glad I'm in love. It's wonderful. I was so tired of doing it for my complexion's sake."

"Well, go on," put in Miroslava. "How'd it end?"

"Well, he gave me this perfectly dreadful awful salacious corrupt wicked old French smile and said would I like to come to confession the next day at St. Monique's in Marseilles, where he was the priest. I said I would, but I didn't."

"More fool you!" giggled Maude Anne, closing the polish bottle and studying her fingers.

While they chittered and chattered, the tour bus had pulled up and parked down by the gatehouse, and now the driver was shepherding a motley crew of some fifteen people toward the house. Among them were three young men from Milwaukee, lusty youths with pleasant rosy faces, bursting out of their clothes, ready for anything. One of them, Chapman, had already noted the group on the porch. And had pricked up, one might say, his ears.

His two companions had been taken over by an Art Historian, a lady from the Bolling Institute of Arizona, who was preparing a tome called *Latter-Day Variations in the American Palladian Style, 1798-1807.*

"I knew about *Fontanelle,*" she said. "But, of course, it was never open to the public even if you could find it out here in the backwoods. There's an octagonal room upstairs I've waited to see all my life!"

"Sure . . ." they said, cautiously.

She looked at them through glasses like the bottoms of 18th century vinegar bottles. "In America," she enunciated, "there's very little *real* Palladian—*even in Virginia,* if you know what I mean!"

"Ah, yes . . ." they said.

"You've seen the houses on the Brenta, of course?"

"No, no!" they cried, almost too readily.

"Anyway," she sighed, mopping her brow with a wadded-up handkerchief. "Here we are, at last. Here's *Fontanelle*."

"We made it," they laughed, relieved.

But Chapman wasn't with them. He was moving slowly ahead of the group, his attention fixed on the group on the veranda: already he had caught a flash of something in the air. Erotic shimmers.

His friends, Chuck and Carly, sauntered up beside him.

"Looka there, see what I see?" asked Chuck, peering at the three girls on the veranda, who hadn't yet noticed the tour group. They were still in France.

"Well, that's a picture, isn't it?" said Carly. They moved on, but the guide was waving for them to join the others, that the tour began with the spring and garden. Chuck and Carly obediently went back to the others, but Chapman didn't even glance back. He moved on toward the veranda. The girls were laughing again; Pee-Wee had stopped rocking and was leaning forward, making a face, telling something outrageous. Miroslava sipped her highball and guffawed between each sip.

Chapman registered the multitudinous sensual vibrations, as obvious as heat shimmers, and lusted at once.

"Excuse me," he said, already on the top step, "but you really do look like a picture . . . or like pretty ghosts from the old South."

Maude Anne gasped, they all turned to him and froze.

They did look like a painting. They recovered themselves at once, but the climate was still exciting, portentous. They registered his vibrations too.

"All too fleshly, sir, not ghosts," said Miroslava and the others began laughing again.

"Dear silly bitches!" thought Chapman, already choosing Miroslava.

"Lord," said Pee-Wee, "while we've been sitting here, blatting away, the tour has arrived!"

"Yes," said Chapman, "here we are. Do I get a special tour, before the others?"

Miroslava had been studying him and at once stepped toward him. "I shall show this gentleman a thing or two," she said. "Ladies, keep the heathens at bay until you have my signal."

They were amazed at her, but nodded assent.

She led Chapman into the hall, gazing into his eager eyes. His blood was drumming in his ears.

"I'm a semanticist," he began, "and I believe in blunt speech. Lord, you Southern girls! I don't know how to begin to pin you down."

Miroslava fluttered a hand to her breast, soubrette for one moment. *"Pin me down?* Do you mean . . . ?"

"The instant I saw you . . ." he began, but then paused and enquired. "Have you read *Eros Denied*?" His hand went to her waist.

"Ah, yes, *Eros Denied,* by Wayland Young," she smiled. "I get your drift . . ."

"What I want . . ." he began, but she smiled and cut him short.

"You want to fuck, is that it? You see, I'm a liberated lady . . . and I believe in plain speech too . . . *and* I've read *Eros Denied*." She paused, watching him turn scarlet.

"Well, I don't like to beat about the bush," he hazarded.

"Nor do I," she said. "Anyone who is beating about in the bushes runs the risk of redbugs and you know how exasperating *they* can be." They were moving up the stairs by now. "And why beat about bushes," she went on softly, "when there is a perfectly lovely four-poster bed waiting to be used just up there."

"What I meant," smiled Chapman, "was I don't like to

mince words. What I want . . . is you. I want to give you the definitive experience . . . a flight, a ride, a game of double-back bear . . ."

"Why, you sweet old-fashioned thing," she said. "And so you shall!"

They entered the huge bedroom with the four-poster.

"You'll have to unlace me in back," she said. "This costume was not created for implusive pleasures . . . and instant fun."

Soon they were in the great bed, curtains drawn.

Downstairs, the tour group had finished the garden preliminaries and were moving up the steps of the veranda. Pee-Wee and Maude Anne, struggling into their lace mitts, stood just in front of the door, their hoopskirts blocking the entrance.

"Tickets, please," called out Maude Anne, brandishing her punch, which was on the end of a long ribbon attached to her belt. The visitors began fishing cardboard rectangles from pockets and handbags. There were six black dots on each ticket, alongside the names of the six structures—four houses, one fort, one courthouse—which comprised the tour. Maude Anne made a point of taking as long as possible, making small talk, asking each one where he was from, pretending her puncher blocked, examining it, shaking it, carrying on. Pee-Wee took forever getting them through the formality of signing the guestbook, turning this into bureaucratic ritual, insisting they write their places of origin, "comments" if they wished. She held the pen forever between each signature.

"Have you seen the view?" purred Maude Anne, leading them toward the end of the veranda. "Through the gap in those live-oaks you can just see the steeple of Bay Minette courthouse. Way off in the distance . . . see?"

By now the Art History lady was getting impatient and came up to Chuck and Carly. "At this rate, we'll never get to see the other two houses," she scowled.

"I'm Dr. Rowena Brand . . . Bolling Institute, Weshanemee University . . ." growled the lady. "We might as well introduce ourselves if we're going to be stranded here for the rest of our mortal lives."

The young men introduced themselves and by then the group had been admitted to the house. Pee-Wee led them triumphantly to the front parlor and pointed out a series of historical scenes which seemed done in odd faded watercolor but which on closer inspection turned out to be mosaics of a kind, made of thousands of bits of cut up postage stamps.

"This shows the famous steamboat race," said Pee-Wee, "between the *Morning Star* and the *Queen of the West*. The *Queen* won, you know," she added gravely, "because the Captain took the precaution of leaving all excess weight on shore: the gilding on the stack brace, his mother-in-law . . . and even his kid gloves."

This brought a few titters from those who were heeding her, but not from Dr. Brand, who had gone striding up to Maude Anne, who was standing behind the tour group.

"I don't see why I can't go upstairs and see the famous room which interests me," she said. "I have credentials, I'm doing a book on Palladian stuff in the United States. The other young lady is showing one of our group around up there right now, I saw them going upstairs while we were out on the drive."

"Uh . . . well, yes . . . but you see, he has . . . uh . . . special credentials too . . ."

"And what are they?" asked Dr. Brand sharply.

"Well, he's into . . . parapsychology . . . yes, parapsychology . . . he's come to . . ." Maude Anne smiled with real inspiration, "he's come to see about laying a ghost."

"Exorcism? That takes a priest," snapped Dr. Brand.

"I mean . . ." faltered Maude Anne, ". . . he wanted to get a feel . . . of the bedroom . . . that's the room that's haunted, you see. He'll be down tereckly and we can go up."

"Haunted by exactly *whom*?" asked Dr. Brand, squinting hard as she stared upstairs, at which Maude Anne jockeyed herself into a position to block the stairs if need be.

"Uh . . . the Lizard Lady," said the ballad-maker, ever ready.

By now most of the group had come out of the study and gathered around Maude Anne and Dr. Brand. Knowing she had her audience, Maude Anne spoke very softly, so they had to crane, and keep still themselves.

"On the other side of Binn's Creek—what we call the bad side, we're on the good side—lives this clan of swamp people named Rudd, who don't work, just hunt and fish and play cards. Must be about fifty of them hidden out there in the swamps. They're mean and they're shifty and kill lots of things for want of anything better to do. Especially snakes and lizards, both of which we have lots of, what with the ruins of the fort and lots of brick and rubble from French times. Anyway, some years back when this house was just a ruin, one day Red Rudd was chasing a lizard, he had a rock in his hand to squash it flat, chased it to within sight of this house . . . and he saw an upstairs window slowly slowly open, creak creak . . . and he saw what looked like a wrinkled little old lady in a sunbonnet looking out . . . she just stared at him with two beady little eyes and he was rooted to the spot . . . then you know what? . . . she parted her lips, but what came out was the sound of a flute, not a voice . . . she made this sound and Red Rudd was so amazed he dropped his rock and couldn't move, unless maybe he really was spellbound . . . but the lizard he was chasing went lickety-split through the grass right up the wall to that windowsill and she picked it up and cuddled it, put it inside and closed the shutters again."

She was making small gestures, illustrating the actions of the tale, but hurrying on, afraid she'd lose her hearers' attention, seeing Dr. Brand was about to speak again.

"Well, Red Rudd just stood there rubbing his eyes, then hurried back across the creek to tell the others and of course they didn't believe one word, just joshed him and said he'd been drinking too much moonshine. But then one day Red Rudd was chasing a rabbit in some piney woods further upstream and he scared a whole bunch of lizards out of a pile of rubble and they went darting off in the high grass and he chased them around that rubble and almost fell over somebody standing on the other side. It was a tiny figure, didn't come up to his elbow. She had on an ole-timey dress down to her ankles and this big sunbonnet that hid her face completely. He thought this must be the lady of the ruined house and went right up close to her. Now this is where it's hard to understand. He says she lifted her head, though he couldn't see her face, and made this soft, sweet sound at him, like a violin, and she put her arms around his neck—she had to stand on tiptoe—and pulled his mouth down to hers and gave him a kiss . . . *Well!* to hear him tell it, the sun stood still in the sky, and graves yawned! didn't they ever! . . . to hear him tell it. Then she went skittering off, with dozens of lizards clinging to her skirt and running beside her. He caught a glimpse of her hands, the only part of her uncovered. Her skin was as grey as pear-wood ash, and he said they looked scaly and more like *claws!* That brought him to his senses. It was getting dark, he thought he'd better head for home. But he felt this strange sensation. His skin was burning all over his body, like an awful sunburn, but this was in November, mind you. When he got home, they all looked at him in a funny way, and they said, 'What's come over you, Red Rudd?' 'cause his skin had turned all crinkly and funny and was a greenish-grey."

Now Maude Anne realized she had command of them all. They were staring at her in silence, so she slowed down, and emphasized when she felt like it the rest of the way. Meanwhile Pee-Wee hovered near the stairs, awaiting some signal from Miroslava. The silence up there was both reassuring and worrisome.

"And it stayed like that! No doctor could tell him what it was. But he got mad and got together three of his close pals to set out here to just have a close look at the Lizard Lady. Red Rudd said he'd beat her hide off and make himself a jacket. They chose the night of the November full moon, and waited till midnight. Red Rudd was carrying a floundering lamp, but halfway along the mantle broke, so they only had moonlight. When they got here, tramping through all the undergrowth—it wasn't lawn like now—they lost a little nerve 'cause they could see there was light in every room in the house. Through the closed shutters they could see a greenish-yellow wavering light, like some kind of kerosene lamp or candles. The front door wasn't locked, they pushed it open and they couldn't believe their eyes . . .

"The house was full of lizards, why in the front parlor on an old sagging sofa there must have been at least a hundred! They were everywhere . . . and the lights! There were clouds—no, I don't mean swarms, yes, I do mean clouds—of lightning bugs. Some were clinging to the ceilings, others were flying about, up and down stairs, for instance, in two currents, one up one down, and lizards running up and down stairs too. Those four men just stumbled in, gaping, not saying a word. But then Red Rudd got mad and put down his foot and squashed two lizards flat. Right away, the other lizards stopped running about and stood still, looking at Red. Then there came this sweet sound, sad, one of the fellows said it sounded like a muted trumpet and they had to follow it, nothing could keep them from moving up the stairs as in a dream, right along to the big bedroom.

"And the Lizard Lady was there, sure enough, in a kind of trailing nightgown, all silvery they said it was, and a nightcap with a big frill that hid her face. She sang this strange sweet note and they all went up to her. First she pulled Red Rudd to her for another kiss, then two of the other men. The youngest she spared for some reason of her own. You know what happened! The two other men came down with the same strange skin ailment as Red Rudd, but *he* began to shrink. His skin began to hang in folds, and after a year he died, croaking something in an unknown language. The youngest, whom she hadn't kissed, developed a stammer and nowadays practically can't talk.

"Anyway . . . a week after this visit, the whole Binn clan ganged up and came to burn down the house with the Lizard Lady in it. Only when they arrived she was waiting on the veranda and she spoke in her musical language and froze their wills. Then she came traipsing calmly down the stairs with thousands of lizards trailing after her and they went through the high grass, into the magnolia grove and vanished. All those trashy Binn people were in a kind of trance, so they just went home. Nobody knows where the Lizard Lady went, but they *do* say . . . that upstairs here . . . on the night of the November full moon . . ."

"Upstairs here," came an acid strong voice, Dr. Brand's, "is what I have come to see, Lizard Lady or no Lizard Lady. One member of our tour is already being shown about; I see no reason why we cannot go up there too."

"Yeah," said a portly man. "We don't have all day."

"I did read," said a prim little old lady with a prim smile, "that there is an interesting subspecies of lizard in these parts called the Fort Morgan Bluebag."

"You are so right!" cried Pee-Wee frantically, as she arranged her crinolines to block the stairway completely. Others began to mutter and murmur, and Maude Anne looked desperately upwards, hoping for a sign from Miroslava. No sign. Pee-Wee suddenly darted to a cupboard by the stair, unlocked it and fiercely yanked out a lyre- or zither-like instrument.

"A table-harp!" she cried joyously. "Brought at great expense from Seneca Falls, New York during the War Between the States! Smuggled through the lines, stained with the blood of Yankee soldiers! Hasn't been played since the day General Lee surrendered! Now it's been restored, along with this perfectly lovely ole house . . ." Here she paused gracefully, and dropped into a deep curtsey. "You are going to be honored with hearing this voice from the past speak again. I've been practicing for months!"

Everybody but Dr. Brand looked startled and for the most part pleased. Maude Anne wondered if she should sneak out and toss pebbles up against the bedroom window, but when the silvery tankle of the table-harp began, she was rooted.

Turning a key, essaying a treble string, *twank!* Pee-Wee looked up and said: "I'm going to play Ashwander's *Jimmy Jump Jamboree Ragtime Polka,* one of our loveliest old S'uthern airs."

"Oh, you darling fake!" thought Chuck.

And off she went, mile-a-minute, twinkle, twankle, plinkety-plunk, nothing if not *scherzo allegretto* and certainly ragtime. Chuck was patting his foot, others began to snap their fingers in time, the big man was grinning. Dr. Brand looked like incipient hysteria as she bit her wadded handkerchief.

Finishing with a flourish, Pee-Wee rose from where she sat on the third step and bowed to their applause, and after a hasty glance upwards, immediately cried out: "I knew you'd simply adore it! Now I'll play something more *melting.* An Italian serenade by Maestro Alfredo Di Rocco, who visited this house with Jenny Lind on her very last tour. A *serenata: Perchè mi guardi così stasera, Despina?*"

After some silvery arpeggios, she launched into the song, plaintive in her thin voice.

"I feel we have had quite enough of what seems to me to be delaying actions," announced Dr. Brand, stentorian over the music.

"Oh, Lord!" thought Pee-Wee in panic. "If I had brought my clogs, I could do a clog-dance. Up and down the stairs!"

"Oh, come on, she's doing us a favor," said Chuck.

"Giving us a treat," said Carly. "We can always go upstairs; you don't hear a table-harp every day." By now both boys had caught on to everything.

"Oh, Saint Rita, help us!" prayed Maude Anne inwardly, thinking that surely Pee-Wee would run upstairs and give warning if the group tried to force the issue. "I know what I *could* do," she thought. "But, Lord, it'll take me six months to get them back . . ." She stared at her puncher.

Inevitably, Pee-Wee's song ended and Dr. Brand, seconded by two other adamant ladies, started toward the stairs. Pee-Wee took a long time gathering her skirts and getting up, managing to place the table-harp smack in the middle of the lowest step.

"Oh, yes, you want to go upstairs," she almost shouted, her head turned upwards. "Of course, we'll all go upstairs now . . . Upstairs!" But she didn't make a move.

"I have come to see the octagonal room, young lady. I have paid for my ticket, furthermore have professional credentials, and after waiting fifty years to see it, I am not in a mood to be entertained by your vaudeville. Shall we go upstairs?!" She turned to speak to the two other ladies as she gripped the bannisters and stepped over the widespread flounces of Pee-Wee's crinoline. Pee-Wee instinctively cringed. The other ladies huddled close behind the Art Historian.

Suddenly there came a piercing scream and Pee-Wee, quick as ever, knew her cue. She rushed to Maude Anne who stood there with her hands behind her, her puncher swinging from side to side on its grosgrain ribbon.

"My God, Maude Anne, what on earth have you done?" she quavered in theatrical tones, "Show me! Show me what you've done!" The entire tour group, including the three adamant ladies, had all turned, bewildered, to stare. Very very slowly Maude Anne drew her hands from behind her and held them out. Cleverly, Pee-Wee managed to keep them hidden from the others.

"Oh, everybody come here!" shouted Pee-Wee. "Right away! Everybody! Just look what this Maude Anne has done!" She turned to murmur into Maude Anne's ear: "Bless you, you're a real friend!" Then she turned back to the crowd. "Just look at what she's done!"

As they crowded around, bending closer to study her outstretched hands, Maude Anne looked over their heads with relief, seeing a rosy Chapman and a rosy Miroslava coming downstairs, little fingers discreetly locked, eyes fixed on eyes, almost buzzing.

The group was fascinated. Maude Anne, for a last diversionary tactic, had punched holes in each of her long fingernails. Everybody was deeply impressed but didn't quite know why.

Somewhere In The Nowhere

I had been on ice for three years, in the Arctic Circle, Alaska, the Andreanof Islands. I had seen the sun only five times in that period—once, happily enough, when it shone for four hours on the day the war ended. I had come from Adak across the Pacific in an old salmon fishing vessel. There had been terrible storms and three days—out of the ten-day voyage—of incredible pitching and tossing. I had undergone a medical examination at Seattle and had been sent to California to be treated for intense wool allergy in a soldiers' rest camp. And, at last, I was given that most precious of documents—a certificate of discharge from the army.

I bought civilian clothes, made a ceremony of giving my hated army uniform to a garbage collector in San Bernardino, California and set out—not so much elated as simply weightless, disembodied, half-crocked—for Los Angeles and for Hollywood. My thought was that finding myself on the West Coast I might as well see our home-grown Sodom and Gomorrah for myself, since I might never find myself thereabouts again. To understand the effect the neon lights and traffic sounds had on me you must understand that for three interminable years I had lived amidst snow, blizzards, totally black nights; I had seen no female, had drunk no wine, had experienced my first earthquake, my first volcanic eruption, and my first plane wreck. And I had known the trembling silence of the Arctic night, bestowing upon one a great gift: the sense of stately time moving in cold space, far from human concerns and dimensions.

So I went as a savage, or an angel, not as an ordinary creature. After the tundra and snow, the city streets seemed alarmingly hard and flat; I heard my heels ringing on the pavements. I jumped at every klaxon, every roar and squeal of passing cars. The sight of so many people fascinated and unnerved me. I was drawn to women, all women, obsessed by their voices and their movements. I have often had a sensation of being estranged, of being outside of reality, or rather of being inextricably caught between two realities, but never so strongly as that moment when I stepped down into the Los Angeles station, which is built in a style best described as Shangri-La modern. There were illuminated fountains, ornamental trees, and from somewhere came a much-amplified voice of Mildred Bailey singing *Right as the Rain.* There were soldiers, V-girls, Red Cross women in a coffee stand. There was a surprising absence of the traditional train station perfume of orange peel and piss.

I had one small valise, which I checked, a pocketful of cash, and no plans. I had a new suit, an ancient soul, and a powerful sense of moving in a glass diving bell through the hubbub of Los Angeles. I was a kind of Professor Picard studying the terrestial albeit seeming-subaqueous world. And there were a few people in the streets who glanced curiously at me, surprised by my dazzled face. Not everybody saw that I was floating in a glass bell, a few feet above the pavement, but those who saw were just a little bit frightened.

"How filthy," I said to myself, noting torn paper, cigarette butts, dead flowers, vomit. "And don't people make a lot of noise!" Three years of snow and silence had cleansed my eyes and ears.

"Looking for fun?" said a fat whore in a mink coat.

"No, thanks," I murmured.

"Looking for a good restaurant?" she asked.

"No, thanks," I repeated, without stopping, but she followed.

"Looking for a job in the movies?" she insisted.

"No," I said, laughing in spite of myself.

"Well, what *are* you looking for?" she burst out. "Trying to find God?" Now I was laughing out loud and stopped to look at her. I saw that she was younger than I thought, and had nice dimples.

"Look, Blondie!" she whispered huskily, and whipped open her mink. She had a chiffon scarf tied around her neck, and wore a black suspender belt to hold up her nylons: otherwise she was nude under her coat. But in a flash she was muffled up again, and suddenly said in a perfect-lady voice, "Go straight ahead for two blocks and turn left." I was mystified until I saw a big dark man approaching and realized the last was said for his benefit.

"Beat it!" she growled. "Here's Carmine!" She turned away nervously, but the man caught her arm.

"You crazy thing," he snarled to her. "I knew you'd be at the station. Get your ass home or I'll peel your hide right here."

She giggled and they went away.

"Two blocks and turn left," I repeated to myself, and thought it runic, so off I went. I had a moment of indecision at a traffic crossing and was almost hit by a huge pale blue convertible driven by an elegant young man with lacquered hair and sunglasses. A white goat sat next to him.

"Two blocks and turn left."

But it wasn't anything special: a four-story building with shops on the ground floor. Bakery, florist, a shoeshine parlor. But. However. Then I saw an oddly narrow shop—an entrance hall thus transformed—full of Chinese odds and ends. It was lit by a single small bulb. The dusty window display consisted of bowls of dried roots, paper fans, back-scratchers, and a jar of preserved kumquats. There was an old Chinaman with a black skull cap and a black sateen smock. He said nothing when I entered, only followed me with his dark monkeyish eyes.

"How much is this?" I held up a bowl.

"Sree dollee," he said. He was sorting letters and fastening some, by means of paper clips, onto a tall screen.

"Do you have any ginger?" I asked, since I love it.

He suddenly burst into hysterical laughter. "Gingee Rogers gone Nooee Yo'k! No got!" Then he calmed down, blew his nose, and said quite calmly, "No gingee."

I edged, shattered, toward the door, but my eye snagged on a pile of rolled papers under a table. I caught a glimpse of red and gold and pointed at it.

"Fancee pape," he said.

"Yes!" I cried enthusiastically. He dragged them out, rolled sheets of Chinese printed papers: yellow and silver, blue and silver, red and gold, all colors and gold.

"No more make," he said sadly. "War . . . boom! . . . boom! . . . finee all wood for to make."

He was explaining that the wooden blocks to print them had all been destroyed in the war. I ended up buying all the papers of course, and that's why my souvenir of California is a swatch of Chinese papers rather than an autographed photograph of a film star or an ashtray stolen from a famous restaurant.

I found a taxicab in front of the shop and the driver eyeing me, so I got in, and said, "Hollywood," and he gave me an old I've-been-through-this-before look of shrewd sadness before we charged off through busy streets. He drove like a bat out of hell. I was dazed, unsettled. The noise and the lights began to oppress me.

"You lookin' for some fun?" the driver asked.

"Isn't everybody?" I sassed in reply.

" 'Cause L.A. is the town to find it in," he said, watching me in the mirror. He was a middle-aged man with a bald head and thick black eyebrows. "Yeah, no matter whatcha want, we got it. If you don't like anything we got, we'll think up something new to do."

"I'm just seeing the sights," I said. "I'm on my way home to Alabama."

"Alabama?" he said, and began to sing *Is It True What They Say About Dixie?* Then he cleared his throat and said rather shyly, "I live right near here. If you wanta stop up to my place for a beer, I got some grand photos I could show you." And he winked.

"No," I murmured. "I just wanta wander around."

"No harm done."

Hollywood is a big fat disappointment, of course. It doesn't have the false-front chateaux and alligator gardens one imagines. It's just a part of Los Angeles. It could so easily be New Jersey save for the palm trees. It's American and suburban and commonplace. I found a corner drugstore inviting and went in: I had forgotten all about the gear and tackle, the multifarious *things* of civilized life.

"What are you looking for?" the young clerk asked exasperatedly, after I had fondled olive pitters, and had opened several ice buckets and looked inside.

"I'm looking for Hollywood," I heard myself say.

"Are you an actor?"

"No, I'm just a . . . passerby," I said. He seemed puzzled and didn't speak again until I bought a cheap fountain pen to appease his sense of outraged merchandising. Then, after counting out my change, he turned a faintly freckled blond face to me and said shyly, "I get off in twenty minutes—maybe you'd like to come up to my place for a drink?" Then he added, eyes downcast again, "I live all alone."

I reflected that either California was full of lonely people or else everybody now saw that I was in a glass bell, from another planet, returned from the Ice Age, a ghost, a spirit wandering. They wanted to bring me in, out of the weather. Or perhaps my blankness—I was a solemn cipher—was neutral and colorless, an inviting tabula rasa, and on it everyone projected his desire, his dream. Like, I thought with a mental hiccup, like onto the Silver Screen.

"Well, thanks . . . " I began my refusal, but everything was turned topsy-turvy by the entrance of Estelle. She stormed in recklessly, a blondined woman of forty in a black linen dress. She wore one string of real pearls and two strings of false. A cigarette dangled. Heels snapped on the linoleum. Charm bracelet crashed on the glass counter.

"What's the antidote," she growled, "for an overdose of mascara?" She stared me up and down, although she addressed the clerk.

"I don't . . . " began the clerk.

"Look!" she cried, prying up an eyelid. "I'm *inflamed*! Look at that eyeball! It comes from the mascara, you can bet your boots. What have you got for it?"

"I'd try boric acid," he said coldly.

"Boric acid, shit!" she muttered. "I want something in a pretty bottle with a pretty top."

"Well, there's *Eve-Tone*," he said.

"No, gimme the boric acid," she said languidly, already bored with the problem and fishing in her purse. She glanced suddenly at me.

"Just outa the army, aren't you?"

"Yes . . . "

"Where'd you serve?"

"Alaska and the Aleutians."

"Cold!" she screamed. "As a witch's tit!"

"And then some."

"Where you from?" she enquired.

"Alabama."

"I'm from Old Lyme, Connecticut. It's a nice name, isn't it? Like a drink. If you were in uniform," she smiled suddenly and revealed a nest of wrinkles around her eyes, and neat white teeth, "I'd buy *you* a drink, but now that you're a civilian, you'll have to buy *me* one. Come on!" She seized my arm and off we went.

We climbed down into a battered low sports car and zoomed off. Again I was amazed at the cozy air of Hollywood. Colonial cottages where I looked for opium dens, perennial borders where I hoped for the Garden of Allah. We pulled up to a curb-service bar where waitresses alarmingly costumed as cowgirls brought us double whiskeys in blown Venetian glasses.

"Are you in movies?"

"Ah," she said sadly. "I knew you'd ask that question." She smoothed back her blond locks. "It's a long story . . . "

And it was, too. It was three double-whiskeys long. It was about the sensitive little actress from New York arriving in Hollywood. Her trials and tribulations. Her first important part. Her marriage with a man who refused to let her have a career. How, while he was away in the army, she nervously accepted a come-back role in a prestige film, and how, on the day she began work on the set, she received a wire telling her that her husband was killed in battle—just the day before the war ended.

It had been, she thought, a blow of destiny, a punishment for her breaking faith . . . and now . . . alone, always alone, always unhappy . . . and how nobody understood.

"I'm sorry," I said helplessly, burying my nose in my whiskey. But then she looked up to see the effect of her story.

Bad timing. If she had waited one instant I'd have been deceived. But I wasn't. She was a self-dramatizing liar. I must have looked dubious, for she sighed: "I don't know why I'm telling you all this. But it helps to talk to people. We're all in this fight together."

"This peace," I corrected. "Remember?"

"Ah, yes," she said sadly, then added suddenly, "What's in that roll you're carrying?"

"Chinese papers."

"*Chinese papers*? What for?"

"Oh, to cover books . . . or things like . . . "

"Chinese papers! Where'd you get them? You don't look like the type to have Chinese papers, if you ask me." She studied me seriously. "But nowadays you can't tell."

I chuckled.

"When I was a little girl I had a Chinese nurse," she began. "She tried once to steal me; she was in the stolen babies ring."

No more, I thought, so I said, "Let's move on, hunh?"

"Oh," said Estelle, "I can't ask you to my place just now. My . . . brother . . . is staying with me . . . but tomorrow afternoon . . . "

"Doesn't matter," I said, paying the cowgirl. "Let's go have another drink somewhere, and eat supper."

"Okay," she said. "Just wait a minute." And went inside. I got out of the car to stretch my legs and to stare up at the starry sky. I was homesick for the Aleutian Islands and felt I'd been cheated of something. I felt it was all a mistake, my yearned-for glitter and excitement of civilization was not what I wanted, after all. I thought of friends who'd been killed in the war, and thought how destiny is a strange idiot, at best. Suddenly I kicked up my heels and ran—I couldn't stand any more of Estelle, I had to be alone. I slowed to a walk after a moment and thought, "Two blocks and turn to the left."

Which turned out to be a curved drive with a barrier like a train crossing. But the barrier was up and I strolled in, past stucco bungalows and hollyhock gardens. I passed a huge estate with a French iron grille and statuary, and arrived at what I thought was the scene of a fire. There were trucks, an ambulance, police, people milling about a ruined house. Then I saw that it wasn't a ruined house, only a partially built one, and I realized that I'd found Hollywood: a scene was being "shot." There was much screaming and turning off and on of lights. I couldn't grasp the import of the scene: a woman in black comes out the front door, leading a child. A man appears at the window and threatens her with gestures of violence. That was all: I grew hypnotized to see it repeated again and again. Finally I climbed up onto a coil of cable to have a better view. A big sandy policeman came over to me, signalling for me to get down.

"What do you think you're doing?"

"Looking," I said.

"Well, that's a reasonable answer."

"What's the film?"

"I don't know."

"But haven't you . . . "

"How'd you get in?" he interrupted. "This is a closed set."

"Came down that street."

"Nobody stopped you?"

"No."

"What's in that roll?"

"Chinese papers."

"Chinese papers, hunh? Can you read Chinese?"

"No."

"I can, a little. But what are you up to? Just been discharged, hunh? New shoes, new suit, the dazed look. Where'd you serve?"

"Oh . . . Alaska and the Aleutians."

"Cold, hunh? And now you're hot. Just a thing let loose."

I only smiled, but he went on.

"Looking for fun, hunh? You wanta have some fun?"

"Well, you see . . . "

"If you wanta come up to my place tomorrow afternoon . . . we could make things happen . . . "

"But . . . you see . . . "

"Oh, I get it. You're konked by the uniform. I'll tell you a secret: I'm not a cop. I'm an actor. Oh, I play in the film all right, but tonight I'm doing real life drama. They got me in uniform doing guard duty, 'cause all the real cops are off at a ju-jitsu conference."

"I see. But . . . "

"Come on, don't give me the shy-boots routine. You're human, aren't you?"

"I hope so!"

He laughed, and placed a huge paw on my shoulder. "You see, Owly, I'm already booked for tonight. But tomorrow is another day."

"I may not," I said softly, "recover from this one. It's my first time in Hollywood."

"Hollywood, Gollywood," he chuckled. "Never a dull moment. Want a vitamin pill?" He pushed a *repoussé* silver case toward me.

"No, thanks."

He gulped down a couple and jammed the case in his pocket.

"There's my replacement," he said, indicating another man in police costume, to whom he waved a greeting. "Now I'm off."

As if on cue, the battered sports car roared up just then. Estelle.

"It's my wife," he said. "She's come to keep me out of mischief. She has plans for tonight. But if you wanta come by here after lunch tomorrow, I know a nice quiet place. I'm not really queer, you understand, just warm-natured. Besides, fun's fun!"

Estelle was introduced and we shook hands like perfect strangers. They gave me a lift into town and we chatted.

"Just outa the army?" Estelle asked.

"Uh . . . yes," I said, startled.

"Where'r you from?" she enquired quite seriously.

"Alabama."

"Estelle is from Richton, Mississippi," said Jack. "Ever hear of it? It's too small to show on the map."

"Go to hell," said Estelle.

"You'd never guess what she does in this world," said Jack.

"Gosh, no!" I said with almost too great an emphasis.

"She's a tapestry mender."

"I studied in France before the war."

"You get a lot of work?" I demanded.

"There are more Gobelins right here in L.A. than you'd dream," she said, almost hurt.

Now we arrived at the place I'd indicated, near the station, and Jack got out to let me out. Estelle, at the wheel, turned a wicked smile at me. I waited, braced, for the sphinx question.

"What the hell," she intoned, "have you got in that package?"

"It's my hair shirt," I answered, "and it's rolled up in a great big map of California."

"Interesting!" she cooed. But she smiled a childish, mischievous smile. I realized that I was just beginning to learn how to play the game. Jack shook hands and whispered, "Same place tomorrow, just after lunch. We'll fly to the moon." Then he winked. Oh, a wink. If I had to make a soundtrack for that wink, I'd record bronze cathedral doors closing, or the *blup*! an ocean liner makes as it sinks, or best of all, the crash of an avalanche in the Alps. But I was thinking how oddly fleshless was all this suggestion of wild amours. Hollywood politeness, crazy-mad, eternal teen-agers panting and groping, and behind it all solemn organ music and voices calling across the canyons: "Even locked in each other's arms, we're still not safe. But the planet's cooling, ducky, so come inside, come to bed!"

When I walked into the station there was an old Chinese woman in a dark blue silk robe selling copies of a newspaper called *Consolation,* which is published by a religious sect. She held one out to me.

"*Consolation*!" she cried. "Japan ruined by the Devil!" *Consolation*! *Consolation*!"

But I was already running to catch the express train to San Francisco.

Love With A Drum

I am thinking of those French clocks which are surmounted by a figure of naked Cupid with a drum. On the hour, a mysterious whirring is heard, and he raises his drum-stick to sound a rataplan; only, instead—mischievous bells chime.
Dr. S. Willoughby
Vues d'Optiques (1926)

The world was living in a great clear globe of heat. Lily Maude sat under the thick masses of an oak tree and peered down the road, shading her bright eyes with an ancient vellum hand. The sun was high in the heavens and the sky cloudless. It seemed the world was poised for some great happening. On the road, in the still air, hung several thin white veils of dust which had been kicked up by a mule that an old man had dreamily led past earlier.

Lily Maude watched them settle. They formed, she mused, a little graph of her life: the delicate ardors of youth resolved into a long slow settling, then suspension and stillness. With a great effort she tried to collect her thoughts, but the sun had crazed them, and they seemed as shifty and soft-edged as the freckled coins of light that danced under the trees, slipping though the rich foliage and moving even when the trees seemed still.

She shook her white head and said "Mmmmmmm" to herself, her lips firmly closed. She was trying to see this road, this sky, this summer world with new purpose and resolution. It was her favorite pastime. Sometimes for hours she'd sit and stare at a pine tree trying to find in its trunk the particular violet tint her preferred painter used in his views of pine woods. Or she'd sit at her white oilcloth kitchen table shelling field peas and watching the familiar little view out her window: fig tree, crepe myrtle, hen house, sky.

Would this view turn upside down? she wondered.

Its lineations were engraved on her brain but she waited for the Demon of Newness to appear. In her heart she prayed always to find the unfamiliar in the familiar: she loved thunderstorms for this reason, when tumbling ink-blue clouds let a sulphurous light escape unexpected from odd corners of the sky to bathe her yard with baleful glory, and make her think poetry or prophecy had claimed the regulated world and was staring hard into the world's face and demanding Why? Why? Why?

A trick of memory carried her suddenly backward in time to her childhood and she thought of riding the *Bay Queen* to Daphne and of how the ladies strolling up the rosy clay road from the landing held their hats with one hand, and tried to keep the wind from blowing their cotton dresses over their heads, their sashes fluttering in every direction.

It was a butterfly crazily crossing the road, zigzagging the air, dazzling yellow against the cedar and callicarpa behind him. Lily Maude watched him openmouthed. The road was so hot and still that his appearance had the importance of thunder or music and seemed to focus thought. For he broke the spell. She shook herself awake and remembered her purpose. The knobby roots of the oak were paralyzing her bottom, so she stood and pulled at the voile dress sticking to her back.

She was waiting for Billie Rundel. Oh, Billie Rundel! The thought of the persnickety face that went with that name made Lily Maude pull down the corners of her mouth and suck in her cheeks. It was Billie Rundel, of course, who had poisoned Tan-Tan. Tears came to Lily's eyes. She remembered his wheezing cough, the glazed eye. Only when she had lifted his furry paw and found a cockleburr had her grief come full vent. Tan-Tan dead with a cockleburr stuck to his limp paw! She had howled.

"Old age," said young Doctor Pipes. But Lily Maude knew better.

Who had tossed peach pits at Tan-Tan that Sunday at the Pumping Station? Who told the postmistress that Tan-Tan was vicious? Well over ten years old and strictly a house pet! And didn't Annie Catherine Raines see Billie Rundel conferring with the druggist back in the back, where suntan lotion stays in winter, instead of in the space between Putnam dyes and fountain pens where anybody else would take a prescription to be filled? Now Billie Rundel couldn't look at Lily Maude and had to wait till afternoon to go in Greer's for groceries.

Lily Maude peered down the road. Nobody coming but a little breeze. She watched it, then giggled suddenly because when she stuck out her neck a drop of perspiration went rolling down the small of her back.

But her mind, which she had come to regard as a mysteriously separate unity in her skull, would only tease her now; refused to take in the road, the trees, the sky. I'll trick the fox by adding up all the details, Lily Maude said to herself: the road is white, being made of ground oyster shells, and all the clover and Johnson grass alongside it is stained with pearly dust, as though dipped in milk. Those yellow flowers (nasty!) are called by little girls *pee-in-the-beds* and by little boys *piss-in-the-beds* (oh the sexes are widely divorced!)

and to pick them is to sleep in wet coverlets, though by what magic these bright flowerets could thus discomfort their ravishers remained always inexplicable. Lily Maude would still never pick one though. That shrub, the sweetpepper, is . . .

Buzz! A gnat. Lily Maude waved her hand before her face and looked down the road again. Would Billie Rundel never come? Billie Rundel was always late. Even as a child if her mama started her off for some place she'd dream and dawdle, then have to run to be on time. But Billie Rundel never really learned to run. Oh no, she'd hop, she *always* hopped like a silly bird, puffing and panting. She never learned to throw either, not really. She only "chunked" with an awkward gesture, her hair in her face, never really looking for fear she might really hit what she aimed at, and that would kill her with surprise.

How had Billie Rundel killed Tan-Tan? Had she hidden all her life's sorrow and pain in a tear bottle (a crystal one from Italy) and poured the bitter concentrate for Tan-Tan as a sibylline gesture, removing the sweet-eyed beast from a galling world of humans? Had Tan-Tan, the known emissary of Lily Maude, looked up into Billie Rundel's eyes which she never permitted of any living creature (indeed had often turned her mama's picture to the wall) and died for his impudence?

"Hold up your head, Billie. Take your hair out your eyes, Billie Rundel." If she had a silver dollar for every time she'd heard those words, Billie Rundel could pave Dauphin Street from the river to Termite Hall.

But she has killed Tan-Tan and she herself must die. With this umbrella, thinks Lily Maude, holding tight to the heavy cloisonné handle, I can bash her birdy skull and kill her instantly. Her heart was pounding and a spider weaving in her stomach. Drops of sweat rolled like detoured tears down her cheeks, her wrists, her ankles. The heat was fierce.

She struck at the oak roots with the tightly wrapped umbrella and tore off a bit of bark. Then a breeze reached her; she lifted her face to receive it. It tugged playfully at the tiny curls on her forehead, making her think of her hair in curlers for her seventeenth birthday. How beautiful she had been! But mirrors feared her now, ah yes.

"Le fond de l'air est frais!" she crooned, *"Le fond de l'air est frais."* Ah, Miss Oleta McAuley teaching French and piano; her grave long lost in wild onion and rain-lillies back of St. Stephen's. The last-Friday-'fore-Christmas was Miss Oleta's private holiday and even now, fifty years later in hot summer, the vision of wooden sabots filled with star-shaped fondants caused in Lily Maude's breast the sweetest of wild alarms. She wished for one, to nibble. Oh, and curtains pulled in broad daylight, candles lit and music playing—Lily Maude could still hum *Jacquenetta* and *Pearly Dew Drop Polka*—and finally the drawing of names for presents. Naturally Billie Rundel had drawn Lily's name but hadn't brought a present. Had been too timid to tell her mama she was supposed to. Too shy to speak when Miss Oleta said, "Lily Maude has no present; now I wonder who drew her name?" But they all knew it was Billie Rundel, because she stood there dressed in pleated blue wool, her legs like a sparrow's, and burst into tears, screamed and hid her face. Wouldn't be comforted. Ran got her plaid hat and ran home while Miss Oleta was digging in her desk and mumbling, looking for a present for Lily Maude.

Now she sat by the road waiting to kill Billie Rundel, who'd undoubtedly be too shy to die. Humming *Pearly Dew Drops Polka* to herself thin and high, like a crazed fife, with the sun bearing down and her bertha stuck to her back.

"Why Lily, I do declare! Have you gone stark raving, sittin' in the middle of nowhere singing to yourself?"

This was the voice of an oracle speaking from the air—no, it was Miss Teensy McCorquodale across the road, half hidden by a fragmentary straw hat, a basket of leaves and flowers on her arm, her free hand in a workman's white cotton glove with a china-blue border. It was this glove enabled Lily Maude to discern the creature, for her freckled skin, faded print dress and general hamadryad air all blended with the trees where she stood. She had come through the Thomas property on a half-forgotten footpath, collecting flowers to press in her albums, with a Date and their Description while Fresh, also their Habitats and her own Comments.

"Hello," said Lily Maude startled out of her reverie. "Come in out of that boiling sun or you'll cook your brains."

This invitation she extended from her oak roots as from her high trellissed gallery. Teensy came over and sat with a small grunt and a long sigh. She held up some flowers.

"Linnaeus thought these two were different kinds, but they are really two forms of the identical same thing. Found some fine ones today. Not so nice as last year though. I have one whole book of polygalas, you know: I commence with the white, then trend into the orange, and finally I trend into the purple. In the back I put the miscellaneous greenish and yellowish ones. But you didn't tell me why you're sitting here under an oak tree on the hottest day of the year."

"It's only 'cause I can't decide whether to tell you the simple truth or the fancy truth first."

"Well, start with the simple truth and work your way forward," answered Teensy.

"Well, what's simple truth for me might be fancywork to you, also vice versa," retorted Lily Maude, thinking she'd sooner drop dead than tell anybody so long a list of reasons for killing Billie Rundel. She shook her umbrella first one way then the other, checking her weapon, so roughly that the catch came undone and folds of black silk flapped first one way then the other, as she shook it from side to side.

"I think you knew I was coming and decided we'd have cokes together."

Lily was silent at this, which Teensy took for assent, and since they'd known each other for over fifty years they just sat there without talking. Teensy kept rooting in her basket and arranging her spoils; Lily Maude staring at the hot white road and heat shimmers down it, until a hoped-for visitation occurred. Two little towheaded boys, all eyes and legs, barefoot, wearing faded shorts, and carrying bathing trunks slung over their brown shoulders, came padding through the dust, kicking up little poufs. As if divining the necessity which had called them they stopped speechless by the two ladies.

"Why," said Teensy, "yawl are the little Martin boys, aren't you?"

"Yesm," they answered, without smiling.

"I've known your papa since he was yawl's size and . . ." her voice wandered off on a high note, which chimed in the air after she'd stopped talking to concentrate on searching her pocket. She found a quarter and held it up triumphantly. "Here. Run up to Greer's and bring me a creme soda for Miss Lily Maude Mayhall, and a Doctor Pepper for me. And what are you going to have?"

The little boys consulted silently with their eyes.

"Or'nge Nehi," said the older.

"Uh . . . Strawberry Nehi," said the younger, rather indefinitely, then looked at his brother. "No, I'm gonna have Or'nge Nehi too."

"Bravo," said Teensy, back at her basket. "Then I s'pose we're all decided."

"Oo-hoo!" cried Lily, "mine has got to be a Nehi creme soda. Don't want any other kind, 'cause they're plain n.g. Mine has got to be the Nehi with the blue stopper. Furthermore, tell Huey they betta be cold or he'll *hear* from *me.*"

"Now what are you gonna get?" catechized Teensy, so after repeating the requirements they started off.

Lily Maude and Teensy—there they sat; no conversation:

a lion and a unicorn holding up a great shield of silence, with the sun brilliant and the first cicada singing.

To kill such creatures as Billie Rundel, thinks Lily deep again in reverie, is no more than catching a butterfly or picking a flower. Creatures of caprice, perhaps only death can prove their reality, these dancers and flying elves who smile and hold the world at bay, imprinted forever in whatever eye they've been reflected. Oh, to be so unconcerned!

But where is Billie?

In the center of the sun's focus Lily Maude was making her own night, like a caterpillar weaving secret silk she was wrapping herself in memories of nights past on this road. Going home from Piero Tassel's when Piero had played Haydn and Schumann for them on a moonlight night. Everybody drunk on music and sweet olive and Piero's famous punch. Everybody silent on a road washed bright as day by moonlight.

But not Billie Rundel; her mouth had worked feverishly, scolding like a jay to an unwelcome pigeon.

"Tomorrow I'm supposed to go tend poor Mama-an'-Papa's grave and I'll hardly be able to rise with the sun. But I *have* to, *anyway*, 'cause the Johnson grass has moved right in and taken over. Nut-grass, too; don't you hate it?"

"That's Billie just spoiling this beautiful moonlight night. Why doesn't she hang up?"

Lily Maude's triumph, then—for that came from Tom Beaufort, walking with Lily and voicing an opinion of Billie Rundel, if you please, who gets nervous now for fifty years when Tom looks at her. His eyes have deep shadows underneath them, always have—Billie thinks he's part Byron and part Red Rover and she likes that. But that's also why she didn't marry him, if he asked, though no one knows.

Then Lily realized she was still singing *Pearly Dew Drops Polka*. More doors opened and she and Billie are all in white with yellow Marechal Niels stuck in their sashes, arm in arm going home from Dr. Billy Du Mont's house. Moonlight, moonlight. Oh what year was that? How did so many summers pass? Is it really forty years since David Krief married that little wall-eyed Stevenson girl? The heart-shaped box with gold paper braid that contained the piece of his wedding cake is still in my attic, thought Lily. When I shake it I hear the petrified crumbs rattle inside, for I would never open, shall never open it.

Billie Rundel, all in white, her skinny legs hidden, her eyes bright. When they had reached the gate she had turned and looked for a second at Lily, then kissed her sweetly and firmly on the cheek. Lily Maude's cheek had been on fire all the way home. Involuntarily her hand went to her cheek—who would kiss it now?

"Something bite you?" *Crash*. All the doors are closed, the breeze has died down. Teensy was speaking. "I said: something bite you?"

Lily closed her eyes and there inside the lids saw the vivid outline of the drastically green trees across the road. How she must have stared!

"Miss Mayhall, you kill my soul," said Teensy mockingly. "Are you having yourself a trance today? I only asked if something bit you, and that's surely civil and polite. You could answer yay or nay then go right back to your staring."

"I was thinking of that Billie Rundel," answered Lily, and sat down.

"Why, you mean Miss Airy-Fairy. What's she ever done to prove she's with us on this earth?"

"I'm sure I dunno," replied Lily Maude, "but I was thinking about her just the same."

"Well you keep on thinking about her, 'cause she'll be along directly on her way to Mrs. Riley Jr.'s meeting. They're getting up a protest about Admiral Semmes' statue. Wanta turn him around to face *out* Government Street, like he used to, instead of toward the river."

"Well, God love 'em," commented Lily Maude in that way she has, leaving Teensy to guess which way *she* wanted him to face. Then Teensy remembered that Tan-Tan was dead, probably buried on this day.

"Where did yawl bury poor Tan-Tan?" she asked gently.

"Just couldn't see putting him on the front lawn, where the children crossing the yard would be tromping on his grave all day, so I had Clitus move that little salmon oleander about three feet out from the fence and put him in there."

"Bravo," said Teensy. "That's nice."

Oh hell nice! thought Lily Maude. Nice that my lifelong acquaintance (for I shall never call her friend) has seen fit to poison the sweetest-eyed dog on all Spring Hill. And for why? Perhaps so I must spend my nap time sitting in the hot sun with Teensy McCorquodale and her bale of weeds. Teensy McCorquodale is surely the product of intermarriage, if ever I saw such, thought Lily, watching the happy creature sorting out her pickings according to size and color. Then Lily remembered that Teensy's father, the old judge, was her own mother's cousin who went to school in Paris, while Teensy's mother was one of the three Beautiful McClellan Sisters from Biloxi, all with long chestnut hair to their knees, when they let it down, which they did if you looked at them twice.

"Those girls are too proud to leave a good impression," Dr. Billy Du Mont's papa once said. "But they leave plenty of hairpins." Lily bit her lip. But a voice down the road made her grab her umbrella and leap to her feet.

"Well, I never . . . !" exclaimed Teensy. "You are *beside* yourself today, missy. Just *intractable*. Not that I blame you. Remember when my little airedale Floradora died? I near had a seizure I cried so much. Most people need a really good cry once or twice a year, but I cried myself right out. I haven't been able to manage more than one or two cloudy tears since then."

Unheeding, Lily was scanning the road. It was the two little Martins coming back in no particular hurry, clanking the bottles together in rhythm and singing *Hell, Hell, the Gang's All Here* in a highly amused fashion, highly delighted with their emendations on the lyric.

"Silly, like their paw," said Teensy.

As they came closer, kicking up dust pouf! pouf! with each step, their merriment was noisier. The smaller boy had found a topless straw Katy and wore it, held up by his ears, his eyes all but concealed. The orange Nehi had stained both their mouths and made livid Kewpie doll lips.

"I think yawl are *drunk*," said Lily Maude as she took her creme soda from the grimy starfish proffering it. This remark sent them into gales of unreasonable laughter ending in hiccups and coughing; finally they had to sit down, leaning on each other in explosive shudders of delicious amusement.

"They're very like their father," said Teensy, gazing at heaven.

But already Lily had forgotten them and was relishing the cold sweet soda she drank. The smaller boy watched her for a while before he ventured: "Why did Tan-Tan die, Miss Lily Maude?"

"He was poisoned by a very mean creature whose name I happen to know."

"Oh Lily Maude, you don't mean it? What are you going to do?" chimed Teensy.

"You'll see."

"Bravo."

This conversation proved too much for her, so Lily Maude walked around the oak tree, banging at it with her umbrella, her throat knotted, her tears about to flow. How could Billie have done it? The whole thing was Druidical and aimed at Lily Maude, for Tan-Tan had been faultless. Realizing that never again would she finger his silken ears, she felt a cold pain in her chest.

Then at that instant when the stinging sorrow possessed her, she looked down the road and saw two things: one, Billie Rundel traipsing along like a cotillion girl; the other, that the shadows had shifted the slightest bit and the bubble of noon had burst, the world resumed turning.

Billie Rundel in flounces and ribbons, covered by a floppy hat, carried the silliest basket ever seen on land or sea: a handle pompous enough for a wicker trunk, but the bowl of the thing not large enough for six medium-sized strawberries. However Billie Rundel had something in it (no telling what!) and was out traversing the hot world.

These children, these baby boys—why, they're David Krief's grandchildren, thinks Lily with amazement; then she realized they are soundless, so looked around the tree to see Teensy and they are silently regarding Billie Rundel sailing down the road like Miss Summertime herself, afraid even to sigh.

"Pardon *me*, Miss Frou-Frou!" chuckled Teensy in a low voice.

Lily tried to tighten her grip on the umbrella but found that her strength had left her, that she stood as in an enchanted circle, that the hour of high noon was gone.

Oh when was the time (was it ever?) that they had really looked into one another's eyes? Had there ever been the buzz of contact between them? Had they ever spoken one to the other directly or clearly? Or was their history all a ritual dance of maidens? This was the crystalline bitter ache that fed her fury of Billie Rundel. The world is full of Billie Rundels who move lightly, never revealing what weather lulls or harasses their private minds.

Billie Rundel, oh those legs! Like a bird, like two dried stalks, twin bamboos: it was those legs . . . if only she were in a long dress again, and the road were flooded with moonlight . . . why, then . . .

But who could harm this jaybird, pacing up now to squeak

in a jaybird voice: "Why, Lily Maude, you're looking right *at* me! What shall I *ever* do to please you—eat toads and spit diamonds?"

Troubadour

In the country along the Gulf Coast, in summer, the period of time between the setting of the sun and total black night is full of sweet mysteries and has the effect of making the world with all its traffic stop dead still. Minute the sun slips out of sight, a hush grows, plants and trees visibly relax. This is the hour of perfumes and emanations: moonvines bloom, and pale ghosts grieve at the windows of vacant houses—invisible to some, and painfully visible to others. One smells strongly and suddenly the scent of green grass, of dust, the fecund richness of ditches and ponds; and after, all the white flowers that open at night. Under the oak trees the lightning bugs commence their play; dogs and even children are briefly awed. One feels that all the genii of the ancient world who wait on the mind's back porch could easily, if they chose, break the screen door and run in barefoot, stealthy but gleeful.

On such a summer evening, after a furiously hot day, a lawyer named Tyler Scandrett sat on the front porch of a high old one-story house shielded from the street by four camphor trees and a hedge of azalea bushes. His sister, Miss Jeanie, who kept house for him and who was given to extravagant dreams which she recorded in a gilt-locked diary, was stalking about the grounds with a hose "cooling things off." Tyler, who had long since ceased to notice his sister—they'd lived amicably together for thirty-five years—was staring at the luminous apple-green sky, and enjoying a remote and pleasurable nostalgia. He was wondering how it was possible that so many years had passed since he had played hide-and-seek among the oak trees on Mattison's property. This is the nicest part of the day, thought Tyler, almost makes those smelly cuspidors in the Courthouse possible.

He had eaten a superb supper and had helped Jeanie with the dishes. Now he gave himself to reverie while Jeanie, never still, played at rainmaking in the yard, conjuring the heady smells of wet black earth. Once she gave a little cry and he asked quickly, "What's the matter?" though he knew what she'd answer.

"That nasty toad-frog under the sweet olive," she said flightily.

"Well, you know he's there same time every evening; looks you wouldn't jump by this time."

"Knowing his schedule doesn't make me love him any more than I do, and that's none."

He made a little sound that could be yes, or no, or my! ain't it so! but which was really the ultimate crystallization of an ancient bit of argument directed at Jeanie. Something like: "You know perfectly well it's just a nurse's tale we learned as children that toad-frogs pee on you and make warts; the truth is they don't cause warts in any way—besides which they eat mosquitoes and are very cute too."

When he made this sound (people who live long together can condense a hundred words into the *clack* of a cup set smartly in a saucer, or express paragraphs with a curl of the lips) she just said "Tsk!" with her tongue tipped against her teeth, and gave a jerk on the hose which, was how she boiled down: "Really, Ty, you act so superior 'cause you went to law school in Philadelphia and spent a year in Panama, but

I after all am two years older than you and a woman, I should know what makes warts, and even if it said in Dorothy Dix that toad-frogs didn't, I still could never learn to like the horrid things. I can't abide creepy-crawlies."

Their exchange finished, he dreamed again, and she slank off under the mimosas. He was feeling, somewhere in his mind, that if he wanted he could dredge up some bitter and rather revolting memories to set his teeth on edge. For a moment he let flicker an image of his father's face when they had quarrelled on the day after the funeral, the father white with grief for his wife, suddenly livid at his son. Old quarrels, old moments of selfishness—having distilled the drop of bitterness to make more sweet and perfumed the twilight, he gently put away the past and concentrated his eyes on the houses barely visible through the trees. He could just make out their neighbour Miss Mayhall on her high gallery, fanning herself with a palmetto fan. Soon the street lights would come on, one in a green veil of camphor leaves at the corner of the yard, another far down the street; then the interminable games of hide-and-seek would start. He sighed.

Sometimes the voices amongst the leaves saddened him; he'd sit quietly next to Jeanie (always busy with her own thoughts) listening with all his body to the rapidly chanted "Fife-ten-fitten-twenny-twennyfife-thutty," the muffled laughs, the cries of the hiders scattering through the trees, finally the exuberant "Coming-ready-or *not*!" followed by the silence of the search. How his body ached in that silence, for then he shared the tension of the concealed and the eagerness of the searcher; memories crowded in on him of Tommy Carly, Teensy McCorquodale, the Sanguanetti twins, his sister Jeanie with hair tossing. He asked himself how it was possible to have been so happy in those old days in the grove and not to have known in the heart that one *was* happy, in a golden haze, in a forest of golden trees, in a lost time.

"Even'," said a small, husky voice.

Tyler looked down through the bannisters and there below the porch in the space consecrated to Grand Duke jessamines was unexpectedly a little tow-headed boy. For one long instant Tyler felt the hairs rise on the back of his neck: this creature had surely sprung from the earth, or worse, from memory: Tyler could swear Bible oath that the boy had not crossed the yard. But he was there.

"Good evenin'," said Tyler, hesitantly, waiting to see what would happen.

"My name is James Allison More, Number Four, it makes a rime," said the boy, not smiling.

Tyler strained his eyes to see him, could only make out faded shorts and shirt, thin arms, legs with knobbly knees and a big red mercurochrome splotch on one of them. A portrait of an anonymous child in a Southern summer, framed in a prospect of jessamines.

"Who do I have the pleasure to be speaking to?" the boy asked with a solemn, courtly air.

"I'm Tyler Scandrett," was the gruff reply—then, "but your name will be Mud if my sister Miss Jeanie Elaine Scandrett spies you prancing in her jessamines."

"Oh, my!" said the dignified child, jumping away from the flowers. "And where might this lady be now?"

"Watering the entire state of Alabama. I think by now she's reached the Georgia line." Tyler, recovered from the initial surprise of the child's apparition, was determined to bring a smile to the face of this solemn creature. But the boy only looked across the yard, now deep in shadows, toward the sound of the hissing nozzle and the plat-plat-plat of the dripping leaves. He said nothing and the silence waited. Then to Tyler's relief at that moment the street lights turned on, flaring up yellow amongst the leaves made brilliantly green where the light fell. The porch was suddenly embroidered with rich traceries of leaf and bough; the light scooped all the bushes and garden beds back into their rightful shapes and banished wraiths. The hedge sparkled wetly.

Tyler stared at the child. Light didn't help much. Was he seven years old, or eleven: with his high forehead, delicate ears, and tow-blond hair strutting in every direction at once? Who could say? From whence had he appeared?

"I wanted so much to speak to the lady of the house."

"That's my sister, but you can easily tell me your business."

The boy looked at Tyler, scrutinizing his face.

"May I sit down, sir?" he asked.

"Well, for Christ's sake, boy, of course you can. Come on up on this porch and take a chair. What's the matter? Are you sick?"

"Oh, no, it's not that," replied the boy.

"Are you a Moore with two O's, or with one?" demanded Tyler.

"One O. M-O-R-E. James Allison More, Number Four."

"I know, I know," said Tyler, quite good-humoredly now, "it makes a rime. Mine doesn't; you have the better of me there. But tell me, where are you from? You don't live here?"

"No, sir, I am from Contraband Bayou, Louisiana, but I have been living in Atlanta."

Tyler couldn't think of any further conversation, so sat quiet, still wondering at the dignity of the boy. He heard the busy hose suddenly silenced, and after heard the crickets and katydids.

"Here comes my sister. Exactly what did you want to see her about?"

The child said nothing. Jeanie appeared, pulling the hose back to its hiding place under the Mexican Lilac. They watched her. When she approached the steps she stopped and cried out, at which the boy ran down and snatched up something from the brick paving. It was the toad.

"Put him down! Put him down!" she cried, twisting her hands.

"Jeanie, you're a caution!" said Tyler, thinking how plain-out contrary she was. But Jeanie was always sharp to strangers, no matter their age.

"It's only a little toad-frog," said James.

"Put him down!"

"Yesm," he said, and did so.

"Don't you know they'll make just perfectly gruesome warts on your fingers?"

"No'm, they don't *really* make warts." Tyler laughed at this.

"Who are you, little boy, coming down from this porch and catching my toad-frogs?" inquired Jeanie.

"Jeanie," put in Tyler, "you know you'd be happy to have that thing squashed dead."

" 'Deed I would not, I'm used to him. I'd miss him sorely. And look at poor Lila Triplett: she doesn't have a single bird left in her woods 'cause she goes out every morning and claps her hands at the bluejays. Minute we start squashing toad-frogs we can say bye-bye to Luna Moths and Monarchs too. To say nothing of Cedar Wax-wings. I think they tell each other where they're not welcome."

"Oh, Jeanie!" intoned Tyler, impatiently, in his best court-house drawl, "they's a big difference 'tween bluejays and toad-frogs case you don't know it."

"Oh, not so much!" said Jeanie airily. "Both toad-frogs and bluejays tend to mosquitoes: bluejays get 'em when they fly high, and toad-frogs get 'em when they fly low, and leave us thank the good Lord for that."

"Now you're using my arguments; I'd thank you to stick to the point. Besides, the reason Lila Triplett doesn't have any birds in her woods is 'cause to see Lila Triplett in the early morning light would scare anything away, bigger'n birds.

You said yourself she looked like the ghost of a dust mop, but I say plain Medusa."

"Who's your friend, Tyler?" Jeanie's voice had altered now, she regarded the boy fixedly with her sad eyes.

"This is Master James Allison More, Number Four, from Louisiana." The child smiled tentatively.

"Four horizontally or four vertically?" she demanded.

"Ma'am?" mumbled he, puzzled.

"Oh," interpreted Tyler, "she means are you named for your papa and your granddaddy and like that, or just is there four people in your family named the same?"

"My papa and his papa and *his* papa," explained James. "But they all dead."

"Your papa is dead?"

He nodded.

"What about your mother?"

"She's dead too."

"Where do you live?"

"I been in Atlanta but I'm going home to Contraband Bayou, Louisiana."

"Oh," said Jeanie, eyeing the downcast eyes, and thin limbs, "you must be hungry!"

"Well . . . yes'm . . . but . . . you see, I'm hitchhiking to home . . . and I did think maybe you might be able to give me a little something to eat on the way . . ."

"Why, of course, of course, we'll give you something to eat. We can't have hungry children starving to death under our very noses, can we, Ty?"

"No, can't have that," he answered.

"I had my supper," James went on, " 'cause a real nice man gave me a ride from Bay Minette and gave me my supper."

"Well, in that case I'll fix you a nice lap-lunch to take with you," said Jeanie, patting her hair and starting into the house.

"Have you come far today?" asked Tyler.

"From La Grange," answered James.

"Maybe James would like to wash up," suggested Jeanie, holding the knob of the screen door.

"No-thank-ya-ma'am." Then squeak-bang and she had disappeared in the dark hall.

A light breeze had sprung up, noticeable only as a kind of touch on the temples and by the shifting shadows of the camphor trees. The voices of the children playing in the grove sounded and echoed from far away in the still evening. Sometimes the sound of a door slamming or of an adult laugh carried from clear over at Bonville Acres, the night was so tranquil. A chorus of children were sing-songing:

"Draw a magic circle
And sign it with a dot!
This little finger *did* it!
This little finger *did* it!
This little finger *did* it!"

Somewhere a lusty child's voice was crying out impatiently, "Hurry *up,* D.B.!" James sat quietly on the top step, watching the crazy shadows, somewhat chary of conversation with Tyler. They sat for a long time, silent. Tyler, watching the boy, was thinking how terrible to be young and alone, yet how wonderful to be loose and wandering on the highroad before the world's dimensions were reduced. James tickled his own dusty toes with a stem of grass, seeing how long he could stand it before having to scratch them.

"Is Atlanta a nice place?" asked Tyler.

"No, not specially."

"You have folks there?"

"My daddy was in the Federal pen there, before he died."

This bit of news gave Tyler pause, narrowed his eyes. He studied James' tousley hair and big gray eyes. This casual infant, he decided, has known a life of misery and drama. The boy's shyness, which first annoyed Tyler, now gained his respect: this is tragedy's own manner, he told himself.

"Why did they send him there?"

But then Miss Jeanie was heard switching down the hall from the kitchen. Out she came carrying a bulging paper bag and a tray with a piece of cake and a glass of milk.

"Here," she said, "little boys always have room for an extra dessert, I reckon. And in this bag I've put plenty of good things for Mister James Allison More."

He took the cake and milk and went to work on them, smiling boldly now, and looking less like a pixie.

"It's real good," he mumbled through a mouthful.

"James says his papa died in the Federal penitentiary at Atlanta," Tyler remarked conversationally to Jeanie. But she would never jump at a piece of news: she went on plumping up her cusion, then sat down in her rocker.

"What his papa do to deserve that?"

"You ask him."

James looked down at his feet. "He shot Mama."

Jeanie and Tyler exchanged glances and raised their eyebrows.

"Maybe you'd like to tell us?" said Miss Jeanie.

"Papa was mad at the time," said James.

"A crime of passion," said Miss Jeanie, with real enthusiasm. "Oh, but please understand, I don't want you to tell us less you care to."

"Yes'm."

"Has it been a long time?"

"Yes'm, last summer. Well, like I said, my Papa was real mad at the time. I ran out to the woodshed when I saw him take up his rifle. I heard them yelling inside. Mama came out on the back porch and Papa after her, real mad, and he shot her, and she fell across the laundry basket. Then he went back in and shot Dokie."

"Dokie?" exclaimed Tyler and Miss Jeanie together.

"That was a friend of Mama's. A very nice man. He worked for the Lilybud Cup Company, that's those paper cups for drinking fountains; that's how Mama and him got introduced, 'cause in the beauty school Mama went to, in Lake Charles (she took the bus twice a week and on Saturday mornings) they had a big ole-timey water cooler—Mama used to put her creme soda in there to cool for lunch—anyway Dokie used to come once a week to take their orders for paper cups. His real name was Mr. Harry Jimson, but he had this way of saying 'okey-dokey' that made all the ladies at the Bella Beauty School laugh fit to pop, so they called him Dokie."

James swallowed the last bit of cake and the last drop of milk. Miss Jeanie leaned forward and took the tray, deposited it on the fern stand beside her chair.

"Sweet land!" she exclaimed, "why'd your papa kill Dokie?"

"Oh, Daddy didn't like Dokie being such a good friend of Mama's. Daddy is . . . was . . . a big quiet fella, he didn't talk much. Mama would sometimes say, 'Clyde, if you don't say something I'll scream out loud,' and he wouldn't, he'd just eat his supper and look at her, then she'd scream out loud.

"Mama would say, 'All I want is to have a compliment now and again to make me feel like I'm alive and kicking. It's too much to expect to go to N'Orluns for the weekend sometime,' she'd say, 'but I do think I'd like to be told I look fairly pretty sometimes.' "

"You're telling the history of the world," said Tyler. "I know how it ends; but go on."

"Then Daddy would give her this look from under his eyelashes, kinda squinched up you know, and she'd say, 'Clyde, if you make that face again I'll scream,' and he'd go on looking like that, then she'd scream, and then he'd hit her hard, and she'd run in the bedroom and slam the door."

"Noisy household," muttered Tyler.

"Uh . . . how did your daddy ever . . . meet . . . Dokie?" asked Jeanie, forgetting to rock.

"Oh, Mama didn't want Daddy to ever meet Dokie, but, I don't know, Daddy just found out about him. Dokie, you see, would drive Mama out from Lake Charles and they'd stop at the Azalea Tavern for a few beers. Mama always said she was working hard at the Bella Beauty School 'cause she knew Daddy would raise the roof if he knew about Dokie. But Dokie was more fun than Daddy in a way, I mean he was always telling jokes, which Daddy never did, and playing tricks on people. Mama used to say, 'Dokie, you'll be the death of us all,' and he *was*, him and Mama at least.

"When Daddy went on night shift, Dokie would come to see Mama sometimes, and they'd sit on the front porch and talk and carry on till after I was in bed."

"Carry on?" asked Miss Jeanie.

"Well, can't you hear he's telling the story," snapped Tyler.

"He wanted her to go to N'Orluns with him, but she always said, 'Gimme time, Dokie, we'll have to work this out.' Sometimes she had fights with Dokie too. Not that Mama was mean, but she was real pretty and she liked people to remember it. Mama laughed a lot when she was in a good humor, lotta times with Dokie. But once she and Dokie had a big fight, locked up together in the bedroom, and they tore the place up. I think they had some booze in there. Mama made me say it was me broke the mirror of her vanity table 'cause she had spanked me, but Daddy didn't believe her for one minute, and he was like an ole bloodhound when he was after the truth of something. Sniff, sniff. So after supper that night he just marched me out back of the house and looked me in the eye, nobody could fib to Daddy when he did that, and he said, 'Did you break up housekeeping today, or did we maybe have us another visitor that wasn't calling on me?' I just whispered, 'Another visitor,' and he said, 'That's all I wanted to know,' and he went in and spanked Mama with a board.

"After that, Mama stayed in bed for several days, without any make-up on or anything; Penny had to take all her meals right to the bed. Dokie didn't come around for a week. Then one day Mama sat up in bed and said, 'Suffering cow, but I hope I'll never see another stick of Golden Oak again as long as I live!' and she moved all the furniture out in the back yard and painted it different colors. Daddy made her give up going to the Bella 'cause he told her,'Ione you know everything you could ever learn in Lake Charles and more. You better stay home and keep house.'

"So she did. Then one day I was walking along the highway coming home from school and here was Dokie waiting to pick me up, to ask about Mama, and to give me a present, all wrapped in fancy paper, from Adler's in N'Orluns, to take to her. And he gave me a fifty-cent piece for my trouble.

"Well, Mama was pleased as punch, 'cause they was a pair of ankle-strap sandals, color of lettuce, in that box. She strutted around that house all day, leaning close to the mirror so she could see her feet in it. 'They're shurenuff chick' she'd say over and over, 'Shurenuff chick' then she'd trot around some more and say, 'I'd like to stroll into the lobby of the Roosevelt in these and hear people say that is a girl with chick, furthermore in the latest style. No flies on her.' I tell you frankly, Mama put a lot of store in being well-got-up.

"Well, that evening when Daddy was at work here comes Dokie in the front door to see Mama, and she kissed him smack on the mouth and said, 'Dokie you have got real taste and that's something I like in people—real taste—yes, when they have real taste and know what is chick.' Then

Dokie calmly shelled out a *dollar bill* to me and says, 'Skeezix, you go treat yourself to a good time, 'cause I have got to have me a long serious business talk with your mother,' so I went to see Bette Davis at the Bijou over in Chester City and afterwards had chocolate malted at Chester Pharmacy and bought some comic books and caught the last bus home.

"Well, I could hear Mama raising the roof from a block away, with some might fancy whooping and hollering. I walked around the side of the house and looked in and here was Mama cavorting about the bedroom in her blue chinnel housecoat with her hair wilder than wild. And I was surprised to see Daddy standing there, I guess he'd come home from work unexpectedly. Then I saw Dokie sitting in Mama's little bood-war chair, with his hair rumpled and his shirttail out. He looked sick, all white.

"Mama was yelling, 'Some girls in Contraband Bayou might be happy married to the original Frankenstein, but not me, I have spirit. I am an animated human being, moreover, sensitive.' (Mama was originally from Bogalusa.) But Daddy didn't say a word. Just looked. Finally he kinda mumbled 'Hum' and turned out the door. Mama kept on tromping up and down, but her hands were shaking.

"I went around back to go in the kitchen door, and there was Daddy on the back porch loading his rifle. I didn't poke then, I ran out to the woodshed. Then I heard Mama yell, 'Clyde, what the hell do you think you're doing with *that*?' then she sort of giggled and ran out on the back porch and Daddy followed and shot her. Then he went back inside and shot ole Dokie right where he sat in that yeller chair. Dokie never said a word, just let himself be shot, can you imagine?

"No!" cried Miss Jeanie in a loud voice, then collected herself and patted her hair. "Then what happened?" she inquired attentively.

"Well," continued James, his eyes shining, "I said to Daddy, 'you've sure done it,' and he said, 'I feel right relieved now that it's over,' and he said, 'Go over to your Uncle Plug's and stay there,' so I did."

"Weren't you sorry? Didn't you cry?"

"Sure, like anything."

Tyler cleared his throat and sat up straight. "Where was the trial?"

"In Baton Rouge. Then they took Daddy to Atlanta. But Daddy was the kind of person couldn't live behind the bars. Uncle Plug said 'Either Clyde or that clinky has to give, stands to reason.' I don't know what happened, but we had word Daddy was dead, so we went for the funeral."

"Did . . . Plug go too?"

"Yes, but he had to go back right away."

"Why didn't he take you back to Louisiana?"

"Oh, I can't tell . . . I can't tell any more!" cried James, his voice breaking.

"Now, now, now," sympathized Miss Jeanie, stroking his hair, "everything is going to be all right."

And it was, suddenly all right, because he looked up and smiled a little and said, "Everybody's been so good to me, so very good," and fondled the heavy parcel she had given him. They sat silent for an instant, a little embarrassed, while voices of children floated through the trees and the insistent "Commmmmmmmmmmmmme *on*, D.B.!" was repeated from afar against the music of insects.

Miss Jeanie rocked sharply, her eyes intent on a spot in the middle of the air. Tyler studied his rusty hands, his mind busy with vivid tableaux of life in Contraband Bayou. This child, he said to himself, has seen more of life's sprawling energy already than Jeanie and I ever have in all our years. Why, he asked himself, did I not accept that offer to work for the criminal lawyer in Pittsburgh?

"Where will you be staying tonight?" he said before he realized he had said it. "We could put you up here."

"Of course we could," added Miss Jeanie. "You must be dead."

"Oh . . . well . . . you're very nice," replied James, "but I have a ride promised me if I'm down by the college gate by ten o'clock, there's a boy driving to Louisiana. I better start over."

"Hold your horses!" cried Jeanie, and ran into the house.

"Well, son, I want to give you something might help out a little. Here." And Tyler pressed a folded bill into his hand.

"Oh, no, sir, I couldn't, I really couldn't."

"Nonsense, take it."

"How'll I ever make you and Miss Jeanie know how much it's meant to me to talk to you. It's terrible not to be able to tell people your troubles. I never tell people I hitch rides with; afraid it might scare them."

"There, there, we must all try to help one another in this world, mustn't we?"

"Oh, yes, sir. Yes, sir, we must."

Then Miss Jeanie appeared with a jar of small pickles held behind her. "Here," she said to James:

"Hold out your hands and close your eyes,
I'll give you something to make you wise."

When he did, she plopped the Mason jar in his cupped hands.

"Oh!"

"They're wonderful for travelling, especially when you get thirsty on the way."

"I wanta thank you," said the little boy intensely, "from the bottom of my heart."

And he shook hands with Tyler, kissed Miss Jeanie, gave them both a long look, and turned and walked quickly off, glancing back only when outside the gate.

"I can never thank you enough. I won't forget this, you'll hear from me."

"Goodbye," they both cried waving. Then he was gone.

They sat quietly a few minutes on the porch, then Miss Jeanie said, "Oh, oh," and commenced to rock again, rapidly.

Tyler suddenly found the reason for movement, he had not written down the child's proper address. "Shoulda gotten his address!" he muttered and streaked down the steps and across the yard. Had the child reached the corner? He tore through the privet that separated the front yard from the vegetable patch and, careless of greenpepper bushes, ran down a row to the corner of the property. He could see James standing with three other children under the street light outside the fence. Tyler slowed to a walk, panting as he passed amongst the musky tomatoes which hold the warmth of the sun overnight.

"I think D.B. robbed a restaurant," a sharp little-girl voice was saying. It was a rosy fat girl with straight black hair and a sassy expression. She was eating something from the lunch prepared by Miss Jeanie. For an instant Tyler thought that James had been beset by the wild brats of the neighborhood, then he realized that James knew them very well. The other little girl could only be James' sister by her hair and eyes. She was eating a biscuit which she offered to share with a tow-headed boy of four or five.

"Here, Billy," she said.

"No," said Billy, "full-up."

God help us, a whole little troupe of homeless wanderers, thought Tyler. James is sharing his food with his fellow unfortunates. Through Tyler's mind soared a splendid image of a kind of Children's Crusade, beggaring the road from Atlanta to Mobile. Outcasts, he thought, offspring of the country's most desperate criminals, wronged babes, left to travel, as they may, like cockleburs, affixing themselves to whatever kind heart brushes against them. He stood frozen in a kind of wondering silence.

"You were gone so long, D.B., we thought you were dead," said the fat girl.

"I heard you yelling."

"Well, I thought maybe we had to come get you."

The fat girl was eating a pickle, had gnawed it all away save the side she held it by.

"It's Betty Ann's turn now," said she, "you can take Billy to be your starving baby brother, if he'll keep his trap shut."

"I'm not hungry," said Billy, "I'm full-up."

"Well, honey, you could play like you're starved, couldn't you?"

"No. I wanta play hide-'n-seek."

"He's rotten spoiled."

"Oh," said Betty Ann, "I want to go alone. I'm gonna try that big white house. I'm gonna say my mother is dying of some dread disease in Birmingham."

"Don't overdo it," advised the fat girl. "Whud you tell 'em, D.B., to get this spread?"

As the truth fell on Tyler with a mortal blow, he winced and cried out huskily: "What the hell's going on here?" and they all jumped. Billy began to bawl.

"Oh-ho, an eavesdripper!" sassed the fat girl, with a delicious laugh. "Hit him on the head with a pickle!"

And she tossed the wreckage of the one she had been eating which sailed past Tyler's ear and landed *plosh!* in the tomato patch. D.B., alias James, gazed intently at Tyler's face with a long sorrowful spaniel gaze before he slowly and carefully stuck out his tongue. Then he joined the other children running giggling down the street. Tyler watched them disappear then started back to the house.

Cleverness and knavery, cleverness and knavery, no truth left in the world, not even children—his mind churned on.

But walking through the fresh-scented darkness, he finally decided not to tell Jeanie, so he returned to find and bury the pickle. This'll be my secret, he thought. Jeanie has her locked diary, I have lips that are sealed. Tonight will bear thinking about, he told himself. As he started again toward the house a grin began to show itself on his face. It was hesitant in coming, but at last spread from ear to ear till his face was almost luminous in the leafy night.